Journey
Of
Illusion

Jamal Abozaid

Text copyright ©Jamal Abozaid 2009

First published in Arabic 2009

This edition published in English 2011 by Actoprint

www.actoprint.com

Translated by Yassin Klaas

Sponsored by Daker Estates:

www.daker.co.uk

Cover Art, Editing & Typesetting: www.samirmalik.com

Proofreading by: other-eyes.com

To discover more about other-eyes editing and

proofreading services, please visit:

www.other-eyes.com

Dedicated to

the People of Qatar,

in appreciation of

your support and love

of the Libyan people.

Chapter One

After many hours of trying, now exhausted, Samir finally yielded to sleep. He was an educated man who liked reading. He possessed a natural curiosity of all matters, from everything immediately around him to the world stage. Although having graduated with a degree in political science from the City University, Samir worked on the farm inherited from his father. He had spent many months failing to find work that would allow him, in his opinion, to sustain a family. He often thought of moving abroad wondering whether that would allow him to work within his specialty and earn his worth.

He dreamt that he had immigrated to the 'Republic of Illusion.' Working as a correspondent for an international newspaper; covering one event in particular -- the completion of a spacecraft and its celebration in the capital. It was the largest spacecraft built in the history.

* * * * *

Danny, the chief engineer, who had supervised the whole production, delivered the inauguration speech. "Ladies and gentlemen! Upon the directive of our victorious leader, George the Great Chief, and thanks to the support of our staunch friends who contributed generously to finance this monumental project, we have succeeded in building this gigantic spaceship. An achievement that will further advance our country, making it more powerful more invincible.

This craft boasts extraordinary capabilities and potential. It can carry great amounts of people and property, is endowed with highly destructive weapons, and powered by mighty jet engines. It has the ability to run for many months without refueling. As you can see, it resembles a flying saucer, but much larger, having seven decks."

He turned to the raised platform and said, "It is now my pleasure to give the platform to our venerable chief and great Leader."

2

Amid rapturous applause, the Leader, standing still at his place on the platform, raised a hand and spoke to the crowd.

"Great people of our country! I congratulate you on this exceptional scientific triumph! All our efforts realized through sound policy and the assistance of our staunch supporters and friends. I particularly mention here our loyal friend, David, who effectively financed this gigantic enterprise.

Our heroic people! On this happy occasion, it gives me great pleasure to offer my sincere thanks to our brilliant engineer, Danny, and award him the badge of The Best Invention and Achievement in Human History."

As he stepped forward to decorate Danny with the medal, Samir whispered to his colleague, John, "This is a waste of public money. God only knows their true motive for building such a titanic craft."

"Wish they spent all that money on the poor, or the needy, or for the starving," commented John angrily.

After the ceremony, ministers, notables and businessmen were ushered to the newly built Fantasy Palace for the remainder of the evening's celebrations.

Out of all high-ranking officials of the state and financial elite, only Michael, the Prime Minister, was absent from the event. He was at a hospital, surrounded by the most sophisticated medical equipment under close supervision by a team of doctors for heart trouble. Michael was the brains of this administration; a wise leader, loved and respected by his brothers who always turned to him for advice in times of need.

The Fantasy Palace was filled with beautiful bronze and marble statues neatly distributed in spacious, vaulted rooms with long, meandering hallways, and vast, elegantly arranged gardens. Roofed with pure white domes, it was a fusion of the foremost architecture of several cultures and civilizations forming a dazzling combination of meticulous construction. It truly was a masterpiece. The Palace also contained relaxation and state of the art entertainment facilities - monitoring cameras, lighting devices, VDUs, escalators, fully equipped gyms, a cinema, and theatre. The outer walls were made of serenely darkened coloured glass inlaid with streaks of thin silver and gold wires.

The Palace was completely isolated and stood apart from the hustle of the capital. It was protected by the army and security. It had only one road leading to its main gates, tunnels connected it with the other presidential palaces. The tunnels were wide enough inside to fit a big coach.

The Leader began his welcome speech at the Palace, "It is with great happiness and pleasure we celebrate this historic event today. I'd like to seize this opportunity to thank my spiritual brother, Danny, for his supervision of this vast accomplishment. It gives great pride to all of us. On this occasion, and in appreciation of his efforts, we publicly announce our decision to appoint him Minister of Defense, replacing Minister Philip."

At the head of the hall, beside him sat Marilyn, the crowned Queen to the throne, with all her radiant elegance looking as young as the Leader's imaginary daughter; betraying the obvious discrepancy in their ages. Her countenance revealed worried and troubled thoughts even when she threw wary smiles at the audience. Her worries ended when she heard her husband announce the appointment of Danny as Minister of Defense. Her smile faded and then vanished as she felt the scorching flames of jealousy burning into her heart.

She lost control of herself, no longer able to suppress her resentment. She was inflamed by this one-sided decision. She was not consulted, or even informed beforehand. It was not the habit of the Leader to make such a hasty move without consulting her.

"Nobody can ignore me. Nobody! I am the First Lady. They must understand I have my opinion. They must listen," she thought to herself. With great effort she summoned her courage, stood up and spoke loudly, "Danny only did his duty. He was assisted by a team of engineers who also deserve acclaim."

Her words immediately drew looks of amazement from the audience. No one had even imagined her to be so careless as to lose control and reveal her true feelings so scandalously in front of such a host of dignitaries.

The Leader shook his head in astonishment at her bold remarks and managed to conceal his anger. He did not say a word.

Trying to alleviate the situation, Danny took the initiative, "I seize this happy opportunity to extend my profound and sincere thanks to you, our Great Leader, for your highly appreciated confidence in me and your overwhelming generosity. I admit that I won't be able to succeed without your efforts, your support, and your wise direction."

The Leader happily responded, "Today is a great day for our nation. Our jubilation is doubled. We celebrate the accomplishment of building the enormous craft and the completion of the 'Fantasy Palace' which has no rival in history. Let's enjoy our celebration. Let the festivities begin."

With that, the Great Leader took a bottle of champagne, shaking it strongly, released the cork and sprayed everyone amidst loud fits of laughter and joyful cries.

"I'd like to propose a toast to your health, all of you," he shouted.

* * * * *

In their bedroom, the Leader turned angrily to his wife heaping scorn upon her, "You shouldn't have interrupted me."

She stopped unbuttoning her coat, frowned at him, and shouted, "I won't allow you to speak to me like that! I speak whenever I want. I don't give a damn. And I don't care if they like what I say or not."

"But you should show some respect for me in their presence. Don't forget that I am your leader. If you lash out at me publicly, I lose a lot of respect," he replied less sharply to calm her down.

7

"It's your problem. The solution is in your hands. As far as I am concerned, I don't see any disrespect as a result of what I have said or done. I have my own opinion and I will be heard," she responded, still looking upset.

"For this reason then, you behaved strangely towards me. You ignored what I said! I should be angry at all the looks and conduct in front of everyone… Now, come on! Tell me, why did you appoint your brother, Danny, to that position without my knowledge?"

He puffed out a sigh trying to swallow his anger. He paused a little to yawn and went on, "I'm very tired and have a bad headache. It is very late, I need to sleep, and this endless sophistry is all in vain."

"Why did you start it then when you know it is in vain? You're always like that… you stir up an argument and you don't want me to discuss it with you or give my opinion… It's typical of you ever since I've known you— always dodging discussions," was her stinging rebuke.

He didn't answer back and lay in bed ignoring her provocations, feigning sleep to put an end to the argument even as she continued murmuring angrily.

She left the bedroom and threw herself on a couch in the sitting room, lit a cigarette, and began contemplating ways of revealing her request; one she already knew would surprise him. Her thoughts robbed the sleep from her tired eyes: Michael is very ill, he is very old, he might pass away any minute, any delay in disclosing her request would shatter her dreams, and destroy her hopes. She quite often dreamt of a particularly high-ranking position in her husband's government. The golden opportunity was now within reach, she was so close to bringing her wildest ambitions to fruition.

Silently she asked herself, "How would he react if I put forward my request to him?" The matter, however, could not be delayed any longer – what if the first light of the new day brought with it the news of this sickly man's death?

She remained steeped in a sea of deep thoughts, smoke lingering around her from a chain of cigarettes, still indulging in her monologue until, finally, her mind was resolute - to confront him with her request, the moment he awoke, come what may!

With the first rays of dawn, she prepared herself for the event, checked her make-up, dressed elegantly, and ordering the housemaid to make coffee and in an unconventional gesture, took the cups herself to the bedroom. She woke him up gently with a sweet voice full of playful affection, "Good morning, George dear. Hope you've had sweet dreams."

He opened his eyes, slightly bewildered at her coquettish tone, memories of how she had been still present for him from the night before. "Good morning, Marilyn. It's so kind of you," he replied.

Offering him the cup of coffee, she went on, "I insisted I should offer you your coffee myself by way of goodwill. George, I do apologize for what I did yesterday… I admit I was stupidly angry."

He gazed at her, unable to figure her out; he simply couldn't imagine she would apologize to him–she has never done it before. He knew her to always defend herself fiercely; always clever at turning the tables on him.

What has happened to her to change her habit and suddenly become so amicable, so courteous, he wondered. His amazement, however, didn't hold him back from expressing his pleasure. "It's alright, dear. I'm so glad you've apologized, and I accept your apology," he said cheerfully.

"I take it then you've forgiven me, dear husband. I know you are broad-minded and kind-hearted," she responded with a wide smile.

"Of course, Marilyn."

"I'm so happy to hear that from the kindest husband in the world."

She paused a little before she went on, still with her flirtatious smile, "By the way, I've got something I'd like you to do for me, dear! I hope you won't let me down. You know, I always rely on your noble soul."

"Your wish is my command, my dear! Ask me whatever you want and I will do it for you."

"But I am afraid you will let me down this time and reject my request."

"No, no. Never. What is it, dear?"

Placing her forefinger delicately at her mouth, she continued hesitantly, her face reddening.

"My request is… is…" She paused, looking down.

"Come on, dear! Tell me!"

She remembered her mother's advice; don't ever hesitate… have courage and confidence in yourself when you ask your husband to do something for you.

She gathered her words, summoned up her courage and said, "…is to appoint me Prime Minister."

He jumped out of bed, incredulous. He had never even entertained the idea that she would ever make such an over-ambitious request. In a tone reflecting reproof rather than anger, he replied, "That's impossible… you know it's impossible."

"What did you say? What is impossible?," she cried, "Where are your many promises you will appoint me to a high-ranking position? You were just bluffing, then. You've kept all ministerial posts for your brothers. You've gone back on your word and failed to keep any of your promises to me."

After a moment of silence, feigning deep sadness, she carried on, "I know you don't love me and don't trust me in spite of all I've done for you… You've forgotten everything."

"No, I haven't, but it's not your position. After all, I can't dismiss Michael on his sickbed and give you his post. He may never recover. I would put myself in a very awkward position. What would people say? 'He has fired his brother - who's proved himself as an valuable P.M. - only because he had a heart attack and replaced him with the First Lady?"

In a soft, less sharp, yet insistent, tone of voice, she answered, "No, George. You didn't understand. I didn't mean that. I don't want you to fire him, but the doctors, as you well know, do not believe he'd be able to resume his normal life and perform his duties if he survived. Besides, he may pass away any minute... and I would like to succeed him in his post."

He looked at her, still amazed. Letting out a sigh, he said, "I know what you say is right and that his case is hopeless, but let me remind you, Marilyn, it is not a custom in this country to have a woman as Prime Minister. I fear this would stir trouble and provide ammunition to the opposition and their press to belittle you and ridicule the government. Nevertheless, I promise to find another suitable post for you."

"Isn't this a kind of discrimination against women? Tell me if there is any difference between man and woman! Wasn't it you, men, who advocated equality between the two sexes and raised the banner of women's emancipation? Was it not you, men, who encouraged women to leave their homes to struggle against the hustle and bustle of life? Was that all mere slogans? As for people, they'll get used to it just as they've done with so many other situations that were unconventional in the past. We live in the world of globalization, Milord! There's no longer a difference between men and women; it's high time women held top positions in the state."

"What about the political opposition who are just waiting for a pretext to launch a fierce campaign against us?"

"Tell me, since when do you give a damn about people's opinion or opposition campaigns? Don't worry, I'll let my father deal with opposition leaders, he'll convince them to support me. He will not only buy their silence, but also make them bless my appointment. You know, nobody dares to face his anger," she said looking him in the eyes.

He took a sip of coffee and said with a feigned smile, "Try to get me absolutely right, dear! I'm not against women holding top official positions; you know jolly well we have formal plans for that. In the near future, you will see most countries run by women as heads of state, but it will take some time. Then again, don't you realize the burdens and responsibilities such high positions demand? They require exceptional skills and political shrewdness, which you lack."

She changed her tone of voice trying to stay calm, "Listen to me well. You can give me this post if you wish. Remember we were behind all the luxury you now enjoy; your wealth, your power, your glory. My father was the force which supported you up to the leadership with his money and means. Hope you haven't forgotten that."

Suppressing his anger, he calmly replied, "No, no, dear! I have never forgotten. How could I, when you remind me on possibly every occasion? Anyway, leave it now. We'll talk about it in time. I have to get ready for work after breakfast. I have an appointment with your father in my office."

As soon as George had left for the office, Marilyn rushed to telephone her mother and tell her all about their conversation. Her mother commented cheerfully, "That's great. The point is that you have placed your thoughts and plans into his head. I, in turn, will remind your father of it for he promised to support you. I only want you to be happy so you don't need to worry. Don't forget, you are the wife of the head of the most powerful country on earth; you are the envy of every woman in the world. You have that world within your grasp."

"What I want now is to get that post. Michael is in a very critical condition, he might die any minute. His brother Lewis, Justice Minister, has long set his sights on that position to grab it the moment Michael dies; he also enjoys a special favor with George. In all honesty, mother, I have no idea what will happen if I don't get that post."

"Don't rush, my little girl. These things need time and patience. It also depends on your ability to persuade him. Men are naturally weak in the face of women's insistence. I think he'll not forget your father's support and backing."

"Anyway, we'll see. I'll keep you updated. Bye!"

"Bye, darling."

* * * * *

In a house in the slum, Barry lay fighting for his life after a sudden attack by a strange disease, which had rapidly turned serious. His parents had no idea about the cause and they could only look on as their son, who meant everything to them in life, so helplessly suffered from excruciating pain as the disease became life threatening. They were on hand at all times, caring for him as best they could.

His father, Adam, had worked in a car factory downtown before he was made redundant, along with all other employees, when the owners decided to move their factory abroad to take advantage of cheaper labour. They showed no deference to the feelings of people in that little town who worked in their factory for years and were the crucial factor in the success and accumulation of wealth of the company. With himself and all his colleagues unable to find work, Adam was unable to buy medicine or pay for any treatment for his ailing son.

A knock at the door signaled the arrival of their good neighbour, Nigel, here to look in on Barry. Adam received him with a sad tone, "Welcome, dear neighbour. How are you?"

"How are you Adam, and how's Barry? I hope he's feeling better."

"Unfortunately, there's no progress. We're unable to cure him despite of all our efforts. We've asked help from everywhere and for God's mercy. Angela is now on her way to her brother, Brian, who she hasn't seen for over twenty years, as a last resort in hope that maybe he can help us find treatment for Barry. I suspect her journey will be in vain but I let her go only in case a possibility presents itself and to prevent any regret later if she didn't try."

"I agree, I don't feel Brian will offer any help. We all know about his arrogance and his ego. He is so hard-hearted. His reputation is well known, even after becoming Doyen at the City University. But let's pray he will take the situation with a kind and compassionate attitude," said Nigel. He then bowed to give Barry a kiss on his forehead then placed his hand on Barry's head in blessing and whispered a prayer:

"Our Lord, Master of all Healers, we humbly ask you to heal our patient. There's no healing, but yours. Healing that leaves no ailment."

* * * * *

The approaching encounter with her brother, Brian, consumed Angela's thoughts along the entire journey by foot on a scorching hot day. She was driven by hope and wishes, and above all, by her burning desire to save her only son, the dearest part of her heart. Her resolve made her painful journey a bit easier as thoughts and memories threatened to tear her mind apart. In over twenty years, she hasn't seen Brian nor heard his voice. Would he recognize her after all these years? What would the encounter be like? Would he turn his back on her or feel happy to see her and help her with her son's treatment? More than once he had turned his back on people from his own town, some of whom, had been close friends of his from childhood. He denied knowing them or acknowledged that he even came from his home town. Talk about his arrogance and desertion of his friends or acquaintances spread all over his town and neighbouring villages, but this does not apply to her. She was his sister and it is said blood is thicker than water. His nephew is on his deathbed, begging for his uncle's high-mindedness to save him.

At long last, she reached the gates of the university— exhausted, afraid, confused and full of desperation. She tried to walk past the gate, but she was stopped by a rough guard, "I want to see the Doyen, please!"

He gave her a rude, contemptuous look and said in a ridiculing tone, "Do you really think the Doyen has nothing better to do just seeing other than anybody?! Go away!"

Calmly, in a deeply sad voice, she begged, "Please, I need to see him. It's important."

At her insisting attitude, the guard changed moods, approached, gazing at her, and asked her more seriously, "What is that important thing you want to see the Doyen for?"

"It is a private matter. Please, I want to see him," she replied.

The guard suddenly had pity. He looked around and whispered, "He's not in his office now. I advise you not to waste your efforts with this man. He has a heart of stone and may offend you or even harm you. So, please leave quietly if you are here for a request or favour."

His words fell on deaf ears; she stubbornly insisted to stay where she was waiting for her brother to come. She had to wait for a humiliating hour, helped to bear the painful burden only by remembering her son's agonizing illness and hoping to get sufficient help from her brother. Soon she saw a stylish car approaching the gate slowly. Her heartbeat quickened when the guard, whose face changed colour, told her, "The Doyen has arrived... step aside, please. Step aside... hurry up!

Chapter Two

In his office, George started to think over his wife's words and provocations. His memory stretched back fifteen years as he remembered the days when he was just another employee in one of her father's banks, and how her father, noticing his extraordinary brightness and ambition, chose him as the branch's CEO. He had brought him into his tight circle of confidence and introduced him to the elite, taking him to important meetings and private clubs. He also opened the doors for him to become one of the most successful speculators in the currency markets where he managed to accumulate a huge fortune, which entitled him to become one of the league!

He remembered when her father had chosen him to be betrothed to his only daughter, blessing their marriage in spite of the thirty year age gap. Marilyn had refused at first, but yielded in the end to her father's wish following her mother's insistent demands after many rounds of discussions and arguments. With this ambitious marriage, he became the son-in-law of the wealthiest man on earth. Fortune smiled upon him. He became a full member of the exclusive club of the elite men of wealth and influence, and they began to focus their spotlights on him more than ever before. His own ambition pushed him into politics, and aided by his in-laws and some well-to-do relatives and friends, he managed to join and rise in rank in the most powerful political parties. He soon became the Minister of Finance. Later, when he announced his desire to run for the President in the election as Leader of his party, he drew strong support from the influential lords of capital who contributed generously to his election campaign as well as using their political and commercial clout effectively.

Immersed in an ocean of painful memories whilst meditating on ways to deal with Marilyn with her stubbornness and willpower persistent and overburdening demands, well aware of her stubbornness and willpower, he was interrupted by his Chief of Staff, bringing him promptly back to the reality:

"Sorry, Mr. President. I only would like to remind you the delegation are here. They are asking your permission to see you."

"Let them in," he responded. Getting up to receive his guests, he said, "Good morning everybody. Good morning, David."

"Good morning, Leader" they replied in unison.

Smiling gladly, he signaled them courteously to sit down. David, the proprietor of Public Construction Corporation amongst other giant companies, took the initiative and said, "Mr. President. We wouldn't like to take much of your valuable time. We'll get straight to the point."

"Yes, David."

"We've come to kindly ask you to intervene personally to allocate a large plot near the airport for us to build a small town."

"This should be easy in my opinion. It only needs the Housing Minister's signature and I've already instructed him to give you any help you may need without hesitation."

"He's refused to allocate that plot for our project saying it belongs to some villagers there who are not willing to sell."

"What? He refused! How dare he?" he replied angrily. He immediately called the Housing Minister and chastised him with severity. "How dare you refuse allocating the plot near the airport to the Public Construction Company? Don't you know the proprietor is David?"

"I'm really sorry, Mr. President. This land is not government property. Legally, we cannot allocate it to anybody. I have already explained that to them and offered them several other plots."

Still angry: "I don't want to hear anymore of this. This very plot must be given to the Company. Understood?!"

Confused yet compliant, the Minister replied, "Yes, Mr. President. Your order will be fully carried out, Sir!"

The Leader turned back to the delegation, smiling, "Do you need anything else, David? The Housing Minister will take care of your request and finish procedures quickly. From this moment you can follow up the matter with him."

"Much obliged, Mr. President. Many thanks."

"I'm at your service, David!"

After a short pause, he went on, "By the way, I wanted to discuss the presidential elections with you. They'll take place very soon, you know. We need your help and support."

"Don't worry, Mr. President. We still keep our promise to support our friends and allies. Rest assured, Mr. President, we do have our means and no one is in the position to beat you."

"But my opponent is obviously popular. Latest opinion polls show our popularity has diminished noticeably, especially after our government gave the interests of your giant corporations its full backing in the face of strong popular opposition."

"There's no need to worry, Mr. President. What we have at our disposal should easily beat any opponent and we will use that power fully when the moment arrives."

Ronnie, the Chief of Staff, listened quietly. He was close with the Leader having met him as a fellow student in elementary school. He was also a trusted confidant of the President who had appointed him to his post upon winning the previous election. Ronnie didn't like or trust David and considered him a 'walking disaster waiting to happen'.

As soon as David and his delegation had left, Ronnie shook his head and exclaimed, "Mr. President, may I say something!"

"Yes, Ronnie."

"Sir, I haven't seen anyone as greedy as David in my life. His greed knows no limits."

"You're right, Ronnie. But you know, I can't stand against his wishes."

"But he is intent on accumulating such massive private wealth, as if he'll live forever. And, Sir, you must be well aware of the consequences of this on the country's economy."

"It's now too late, Ronnie. He's running a huge financial empire. And don't forget, he is my father-in-law, and he was the one who helped me to the presidency. Refusing him is not an option."

Ronnie shook his head with deep sorrow though did not comment.

* * * *

Marilyn was never one to despair or give up. Unwavering, she seized one opportunity after another to renew her petition to her husband by choosing to change tactics and try a more gentle and endearing approach, paying obvious attention to his wishes, something she had learnt from her mother. This was a huge relief for George who had suffered so soon after their wedding from her neglect of his feelings, spending the majority of her time entertaining friends - the wives of ministers, notables and high-ranking officials, and throwing, as well as attending, lavish parties. She seemed always on edge, always ready to explode and often feigning minor illnesses or depression.

Now, though, she was closer to him, breakfasting with him, lunch and dinner with him whilst endeavoring to remain calm and be caring. Above all, she stopped talking about having children, a subject that caused him great stress. Fertility tests had not revealed good news - that he would never be able to father children - and she just adored them and longed to have some of her own. He was being treated by a group of top specialists, hoping to announce the joyful news one day. Marilyn's fears that she would never become PM grew day by day. She feared her husband would appoint another one of his brothers to this position and her patience was wearing thin.

Her mother had asked her father to leak out news about her imminent appointment to the top position, thus paving the way for the matter to be accepted among both government officials and the general public. She began a clandestine, yet widespread, campaign to muster the approval of loyalists and supporters, just in case, and to curb the ambitions of possible power seekers.

* * * * *

Chapter Three

Deep sadness filled Rhoda's heart as she watched her son, Maurice, packing his suitcase to leave his village. When the moment arrived and the truck could be heard at the door, she could not control her flowing tears as she managed to breathe out a short farewell,

"Good-bye, my son."

He looked at her, unable to hide his own tears and said, trying to comfort her,

"Don't worry, Mother. I won't be away for long. I will work, and soon I will have enough money to get my father out of jail. Then I'll be back to get married, soon, as I promised you."

"Godspeed and God bless, my son. Take care of yourself." Maurice kissed his mother and little sister Mabel good-bye.

"Don't forget to bring me candy, Maurice."

"I'll get you lots of candy, Mabel." He smiled at her as the voice of the driver was heard,

"Come on, Maurice, we don't have much time."

He put Maurice's suitcase beside his seat, pointing to a narrow, ditch-like hole between wheels at the bottom of the truck and said,

"There, here's your seat."

Maurice looked at the tightly cramped space where he would hide until he passes the borders on his way to the "Republic of Illusion",

"How long will the journey take?"

"Around nine hours, sonny."

"God, that's an awful lot of time."

"You must be patient. I told you it's going to be a hard journey… By the way, have you done what I told you to do?"

"Yes, I didn't drink much liquid since yesterday."

"Good, we have a long way ahead of us, son."

Maurice bowed and knelt to occupy his place in the 'box' at the bottom of the truck as his mother was still watched with tearful eyes. Only once the driver had checked the 'box' carefully to make sure Maurice's was truly hidden from investigative eyes did he start the noisy engine and set off for the port.

Maurice began to think of his father and the court verdict, of the heavy fine for being late in paying his overdue taxes. His small shop, where he had labored to provide for his family had been confiscated. Yet, the money from the ale of the shop had not been enough to pay the fine, resulting in him being held imprisoned until the fine was paid. Maurice had had to leave college and find a way to raise the funds to get his father out of jail.

The truck arrived at the seaport and joined the queue for heavy goods vehicles. Fortunately, there were only two trucks before them and, before too long, a customs officer approached and asked the driver,

"Your passport and truck's papers, please."

"There you are, my passport, car's papers, insurance, and bill of loading."

"What are you carrying?"

"Fruit. Only oranges and apples."

"Anybody else on the truck?"

"No, nobody."

"Did you stop at a petrol station or a rest area on the way?"

"Yes, I filled up the fuel tank at the nearby station."

"Did you make sure nobody sneaked into your truck?"

"Yes, I made absolutely sure!"

"Well. If I discover somebody hiding in the truck, you know you will face imprisonment and a heavy fine in addition to the confiscation of your vehicle."

"Yeah, I know."

The officer walked slowly around the truck, his eyes carefully checking every inch until he got to the place where Maurice was hiding. He stopped there, his attention drawn by the box at the bottom of the truck, bent to check it and asked the driver,

"What is this?"

"It is my kit box, you know, repair tools, spanners, wrenches, pliers, screwdrivers, things like that."

"Open it, please."

Maurice was listening, trembling with fear. And when he looked through a tiny little hole by his face, he saw the officer's boots fixed firmly on the spot by the box. His anxiety grew so great that he feared the officer might hear his racing heartbeat.

* * * * *

A luxurious black car approached the gate. On the back seat sat a gentleman in a black suit, white shirt, and a red tie, his eyes hidden behind wide black sunglasses.

The guard shouted to Angela,

"I told you to go away. Please, get out of the way."

But she didn't heed his orders. She seemed unable to hear him as she stood transfixed in astonishment, gazing at the car's windows trying to identify who was inside as so many emotions welled up inside her. There sat her brother, her brother who she had not see for over twenty years. The only thing that separated them was the dark glass of the car windows.

The guard tried to force her out of the way, but she pushed him aside and ran off towards the car, fearing that she would lose sight of it. She stood dangerously in front of the car and opened her arms wide in a desperate attempt to stop it.

"Get this mad woman out of my way, you idiot!" Brian shouted at the guard.

"Sorry, sir. She wants to see you personally. She insists. I tried my hardest with all possible ways, but she refuses to leave."

Brian lowered the window glass halfway to reveal a furious scowl and demanded,

"What do you want, woman?"

She approached, still gazing at him, still not believing her own eyes. It really is her brother, talking to her, asking her! She managed to control herself and to recover her composure. In a yielding voice, she said,

"Didn't you recognize me, Brian?"

He raised his sunglasses, looked at her with examining eyes, and replied angrily,

"Who are you? And what do you want?"

"I am Angela, your younger sister. Don't you recognize me?"

He could feel his face reddening with embarrassment. The whole world turned round for a moment. He heard her name and couldn't believe his ears. He stared at her in awkward amazement, then turned his sight to the driver. Their eyes met in the rear-view mirror. Embarrassed, he quickly turned his head right and left,

"What? What did you say? Are you crazy?" He uttered.

"I need your help, Brother."

He turned at the guard,

"Bring her to my office to see what she wants."

He ordered the chauffeur to drive off.

As soon as he was in his office, he turned to his secretary, "There's a poor woman coming to see me. Let her in immediately when she comes. Don't ask her a question. OK?"

"OK, sir."

The secretary began wondering; "He never sees anybody without a prior appointment." He's always insisted on knowing the reason of the visit. Then she remembered, how could he allow a poor woman to visit him on the very day the Minister of Higher Education is going to pay the University a long-awaited visit?! Why is he so angry?

Sinking into his lavish chair as he waited for her, Brian was filled with a mixture of rage and confusion as memories and remote pictures of the past filled his mind. How she had hugged him as a little girl and played games with him, and how angry he used to get with her when she made a mess of his textbooks, his notes, his personal belongings. He struggled to compare the girl from those memories with the woman he had just seen at the gate. The two pictures were totally different. The girl was beautiful, sparkling, full of life and energy. The woman he saw today, in sharp contrast, looked old and weak, despondent, depressed. He had left as she was still young and, though having not seen her, her beauty had remained in his memories. This woman today had destroyed all those pleasant memories.

He shook his head in torment. He felt he had to wake up, rouse himself from an old dream and face reality. He had to find a way immediately to get out of this sudden predicament. Then the thought came to him; Was it destiny that had arranged her reappearance on the exact same day the Minister of Higher Education was to visit the University? For many years he had waited for this crucial visit, as it was pivotal to his whole future. What could he possibly tell the Minister if she was in his office? What would the Minister's reaction be if he knew she was his sister? At this point, he stopped speculating and decided to act quickly, to get rid of her quietly before the Minister arrived.

When Angela reached the office, the startled secretary directed her to go in,

"The Doyen is waiting for you."

"How could he ever permit such a creature to see him?!", the secretary wondered to herself as she knocked on the door and let her in. Hurriedly, Brian jumped up to shut the door as soon as the secretary had left. Angela impulsively opened her arms to hug him, but he pushed her away and shouted,

"Why are you here?" He raged.

Shocked and paralyzed by his behavior, she burst into tears and managed to painfully utter some words, her voice sounding harrowed,

"My son is very ill, Brother. He's dying. Please help us save him, please!"

"Don't call me brother. I hate to hear this word from you. Your son's illness is none of my business!"

"But we need your help, Brother, we are poor and we can't afford to treat him."

"Didn't I tell you not to call me brother?"

"Please, please, I beg you. Let me kiss your hands, your feet... Please help me, Brother."

"I am not your brother! It is no privilege having a sister like you. I've nothing to do with you or with your son. I left all of you over twenty years ago and I have burned all bridges to the past and to you. All of you are behind me now. I am not that man anymore."

And then, in a low threatening voice,

"I warn you, don't ever come back here again. Never ever tell anybody here at the University you are my sister, or that you are related to me. Otherwise, I'll have no choice but to be less merciful. Now get out, quickly and quietly, and don't ever show me your face again."

She left his office almost blind with tears and, closing the door behind her, she gazed into nothing, feeling completely lost. The secretary offered help, but she couldn't even respond. The whole world was empty and desolate before her. Her brother had just destroyed all hopes of saving her only child. His harsh treatment was not as painful to her as the realization of having lost her last hope for treating Barry.

"Are you alright, sir?" The secretary asked her boss, Brian.

"Oh, yes, yes. Fetch me the file and prepare the Meeting Hall. The Minister may arrive any minute now."

"Yes, sir. By the way, that poor woman looked wretched. I've got a sense she has a very sad story behind her. Do you know her?"

"No, I don't. She's just a beggar. She asked me to help her, but I didn't like her way of begging."

The secretary paused a little eyeing him thoughtfully.

"What's wrong? Why are you looking at me like that?"

"Oh, nothing. Nothing, sir. You won't get angry if I tell you something, will you?"

"What is it. Why should I get angry?"

"She looks just like you. My God, one would easily say she's your twin sister."

"You know I don't have a sister. Don't be ridiculous!"

"Sorry, sir. I didn't mean to bother you."

With difficulty, he managed to suppress his anger. He feigned a smile and said,

"Let's forget this silly business. Come on, get the Hall ready. The Minister is on his way."

* * * * *

Angela set off on her journey home, her shame, humiliation and destitution combined to make her misery intolerable. Her pitiful soul filled with sorrow and despair. Before her, she could see nothing but her son's face waiting helplessly for his determined destiny, and she prayed that she would get back and find him still alive. Every step made her heart beat more and more violently for fear that she might be devastated by the news once she reached her son.

As soon as her husband had opened the door, she rushed past him to Barry's room where she threw herself on his bed, hugging and kissing him, her heart breaking,

"Forgive me, my boy. I am helpless."

Her husband touched her gently on the shoulder and said in a hoarse voice,

"Easy, Angela. Don't lose faith in the Lord's mercy. Tell me, did you get help from Brian?"

She groaned in a fit of tearful anguish.

"I wish I hadn't seen him. I met a beast without a heart, without mercy, no…"

"Calm down, dear. The Lord won't forget us and won't let us down."

The front door suddenly heralded relief. Adam was surprised to see Nigel standing there.

"Did Angela bring enough money to treat Barry?"

"No," Adam said with an overwhelming sense of despair.

"Don't worry, we'll manage. You shouldn't give up hope. There are some good men who are ready to offer help. I'll call them now to hopefully raise enough money for Barry."

Nigel left, preoccupied with his self-assigned chore. And within only a few hours later, he was back, the relief money in his hand. And a doctor was called.

"He must be taken to hospital immediately," the doctor ordered after examining Barry. "His case is very dire and of the utmost urgency."

"But we are poor and can't afford the expensive hospital treatment," said Adam with bitter sadness.

"Tests must be done at once. We need special medical equipment to make sure we get the right diagnosis."

"Please help us, doctor! Do something to save this poor child."

"Well, OK, then I will prescribe some medicines. Maybe they'll make the symptoms slightly better, but he will still need to go to hospital."

The doctor jotted down a prescription, explained how to use the medicines and the right doses and left. Adam went, without delay, to the nearest chemist and bought the medicines.

"There you are, my son. Dad has just brought you your medicine. Sit up, my boy, to take it and get better sooner."

"Shall I be able to get out of bed to see my friends if I take it, Mum?"

"Of course, my baby. Soon you'll be much better and be able to go out to play with them."

She gave him the prescribed dose, praying for his quick recovery.

This went on for a couple of days, but his illness grew worse. Adam called the doctor again. After examining both Barry and the medicine, he cried in disbelief,

"What is this?! This medicine cannot be used, its use by date expired eight months ago! It has gone off. Who gave it to you? It's bad and may be fatal!"

"Expired? Expired! My God! Why do they sell it then?" Adam complained.

"Drug companies compel chemists to sell them, though they know damn well the terrible side effects they cause and how damaging they are to people's health. These companies are owned by money grabbing tycoons. Pity, the government has lost control over these companies and the crooks behind them who exercise their absolute power with no moral or legal restraint," the doctor explained.

"God's vengeance upon them will do us justice one day. We've spent every penny we could raise on this useless medicine!" Adam deplored.

Barry's health began to show signs of serious deterioration. A week after taking the prescribed drugs he lost a lot of weight and was on the verge of death. His parents, thus, had no choice but to rush him to hospital, hoping to find a kind, sympathetic heart. The warden refused to admit Barry until at least half of the treatment costs were paid in advance. With defeat in their hearts, his parents had to return him home. Angela wept with silent and helpless tears. Within hours of their return, Barry slipped into a coma. Distressed, Angela cried,

"Call the doctor now, Adam. Barry's lost consciousness."

The doctor showed up promptly. He felt Barry's pulse. Slowly, he turned his head looking at the parents with obvious sorrow and helplessness,

"I'm so sorry, the child is dead."

Angela collapsed, agony filling her cries:

"Oh, God! Oh, God! Those criminal beasts have killed my son!"

* * * * *

Many newspapers had been established the last few years that opposed the government's policy of granting, without constraint, free concessions to giant corporations, allowing them to monopolize the production and marketing of medicines as well as commodities. The next morning, the front page headlines of these broadsheets carried news of Barry's tragic death with the editorials full of comments, criticism and condemnation- "Bad drugs kill child", "Drug companies sell gone-off medicines." They put the blame for the death of so many people who were unfortunate to have such drugs administered to them squarely on the corporations. The opposition, whilst accusing the government of being an accomplice, seized the opportunity, using the incident to try and entice the public to vote for their socialist candidate in the forthcoming presidential elections, claiming that that would be the only means of accomplishing "liberalization of the market."

Samir, too, used the opportunity to lampoon the regime in his own column in "Virtue" newspaper, under the title "Corporations Run the Show." No one was spared as Samir accused the Leader himself of being "unable to protect (his) people from the companies' greed," and the government of being "unjust and corrupt." He blamed it for the neglect and the 'let loose' policy that was running the country and accused it of "favoritism toward giant companies at the expense of the masses."

The violent public attack by the opposition media, and Samir's column in particular, enraged the Leader who, then furious, called the Interior Minister:

"Robert, you've got to do something to stop this nonsense immediately. You must stop this vermin from exploiting our freedom of speech and stop this damn 'Virtue' at once. Its editors must be reigned in, in particular, that rogue journalist, Samir Plumber. He must be sued for defamation, for slander, for abusing freedom of speech and promoting anarchy in the country. Other papers that joined in this silly campaign must also be held accountable."

"Yes, sir. Your orders will be carried out to the letter. And I'll bring that dissident journalist to kiss your feet, and I'll make a real example of him."

The Minister promptly gave the security forces the order to arrest Samir.

* * * * *

Chapter Four

The urgent wail of police sirens racing toward the village where Samir lived tore up the silence of the tranquil night. Special Security Squads had been sent on a mission to arrest the audacious journalist. A chopper hovered over the area with its spotlight focused on a house there. The sight of such a heavy-handed use of force in such a peaceful village in the early hours of the night spread terror among the stunned villagers.

Heavily-armed security men arrived and, after smashing in the front door of Samir's house, broke into the house spreading confusion and panic, all the neighbours watching with horrified, unbelieving eyes.

Nora and her children were the only souls the security men found in Samir's house. They awoke, terrified to see heavily-armed soldiers, their weapons fixed on their heads. The commanding officer shouted his question "Where is your rogue husband?"

"I don't know! Honest! Please, officer, tell me what's the matter. Samir is a kind and peaceful man," she answered, trembling with fear.

"Tell us where he is, or else we'll take you hostage until he surrenders. Don't waste time!"

"I swear to God I have no idea where he is. He doesn't usually stay out that late. What's wrong, officer? What happened?"

"Are there any relatives of his in the neighbourhood?"

"He's got only one cousin, Oscar. He doesn't have any other relatives."

The officer gave his men the signal and they hurriedly carried out a meticulous search of the house— turning the whole house upside down looking for whatever clues they could find. They smashed pieces of furniture, cupboards and drawers emptied and everything else and overturned, leaving belongings and clothes scattered.

They collected all the books, CD's, DVD's and Samir's private papers and piled them up in one room as 'evidence'. These were then removed along with Samir's PC to their vehicles.

That same night they raided Oscar's house under the suspicion that Samir might be hiding there. Oscar, too, was asleep when he heard his front door being smashed. He hurried to the door still in his pajamas. Security men burst in, cuffed his hands and began hitting and kicking him in front of his wife and children, who could only watch on terrified. His wife, Alice, screamed at them, weeping and protesting against their cruelty.

"Stop it! Stop it! Shame on you. Look what you've done to the children. Please stop it, and tell me if he was guilty of anything."

The officer approached and aimed his pistol directly at Oscar's head. "Where is your traitor cousin Samir?"

"I don't know. I swear to God. Please don't aim your gun at me, you're terrifying my children. I still don't know why I am treated this way!"

"Shut up, or I'll empty this gun into your head." The officer then ordered his men to search the house and once again turned to Oscar: "I asked you where your cousin Samir is. You lied to me. You're helping him to hide and dodge justice. You're protecting a criminal. That's why we have a warrant to search your place and arrest you."

Astonished and frightened, Oscar replied "I don't understand what you are saying. I haven't seen Samir for some days."

The officer was livid. He held Oscar by the neck, pressed his pistol into his temple and repeated "Tell us where he is if you wish to stay alive, and don't try giving me clever answers."

"Believe me, I don't know where he is, if he's not at home."

Security men came back after a thorough search to tell the officer they had only found some books, pieces of jewelry and banknotes. The officer yelled "Take all you've found with you."

They blindfolded Oscar and pushed him towards the door. His wife rushed to the officer with weeping eyes. "I beg you, sir, to listen to me. I assure you my husband is innocent. I know him very well; if he knew where Samir is, he would definitely tell you and spare himself such insult."

The officer took no notice of her distressed pleas. "Come on. Let's go", he ordered his men. When they left, her eldest child, an eight-year old boy, asked his mother weeping. "Mama, why did they take papa away? Why did they keep hitting him? What did he do to them?"

She wiped her tears and tried to stay composed and be courageous to calm her terrified children, but soon burst helplessly into tears again. The other child, only six, tried to comfort his mother. "Don't cry, mama. When I grow up I'll take revenge on them for what they've done to papa."

"Go to bed now all of you. It's three o'clock in the morning." "When will dad come back, mama?", her eldest son asked. "Tomorrow, God willing. Now go to bed."

The police car taking Oscar to the State Security Center downtown eventually reached its destination, where the interrogation officer awaited him. Security guards bundles him in, still blindfolded. He opened his eyes when the blindfold was removed to face a tall, stern muscleman biting his mustache and gazing at him spitefully:

"You filthy pig", the interrogation officer began. "I'm not gonna ask you to tell me your name, age, address or anything else about you. Everything is in your file here on my desk. I'm gonna ask you a short and clear question: where is Samir? What's the rogue organization you belong to?"

"I don't belong to any organization, and I don't know Samir's whereabouts. I can tell you where he lives and the paper's address for which he works as correspondent. That's all I know," Oscar pleaded.

The officer yelled at him: "Stop lying, you wretched, miserable criminal. We know everything about you and the cowardly rogues like you and your leader, Samir Plumber."

"Believe me, I know nothing about this organization... I haven't seen Samir for days, and I don't know if he belongs to any organization."

"We know how to glean secrets out of people like you, but I advise you to save time and spare yourself the pain you'll suffer if you keep on denying. It's no use."

"I'm asking you, sir, to believe me. I don't know what I should admit to and I don't have any further information to tell you."

"You must admit you're a rogue dissident and that you belong to a banned organization. And don't waste my time."

"What do you mean, rogue dissident? I have never heard this expression... Believe me."

The interrogating officer shouted, now furious. "Are you really a fool or just acting? It seems civilized ways won't work with you. I told you, I've got all the information we have about you and I repeat, denying the charges is of no use to you."

Ominous silence. The officer suddenly dashed toward Oscar and hit him so hard on the face that he almost fell unconscious. The officer pressed his boot against Oscar's head and shouted "This is only a gentle beginning to refresh your memory. Soon, I will use other methods not so mild to make you remember the days of your childhood in detail! What do you think?"

Oscar managed to raise his sight from under the officer's foot; looked at him in a fervent plea for mercy and said "Please, sir, I beg you to listen to me. I do swear I have no idea about what you want to know. If I had, I would tell you."

Furiously, the officer called two bulky guards in, each carrying a large horsewhip. "Teach this idiot that denial as a currency is not in circulation here", the officer ordered them.

The two guards gave Oscar a very painful lashing over all his body, deaf to his anguished pleas. The pain came in waves so extreme that he could bear it no longer and fainted.

The officer promptly poured ice cold water on Oscar's face forcing him back to consciousness as he opened his eyes, shivering. The officer grabbed hold of him, pulled him closer and said "Have you had enough? Still feeling stubborn?" Oscar replied in a faint murmur: "If I knew, I would tell you."

The officer couldn't hear him. He shouted again "I'll give you a chance, but only till tomorrow, to tell us about Samir's hiding place, and confess your crimes, or you'll meet your end by my own hands".

He then ordered the two guards to drag Oscar to a solitary cell and deprive him of even a single moment of sleep. Early the next morning, showing visible signs of severe torture, Oscar was dragged back to face the officer. The interrogation officer looked at him in malicious joy... and then with an evil laugh uttered "I see you've had a blissful night enjoying our hospitality. Now, it's up to you to choose: confession or 'hospitality', our everlasting hospitality. What you experienced yesterday was only the tip of the iceberg."

With blurred vision and a heavy tongue, Oscar replied, still in a faint murmur, "Believe me, Sir, I don't know what I should confess."

"Enough! Either you end your stubbornness or I'll put an end to your life", the officer shouted impatiently. Then, with his rage growing with the loudness of his voice he said "Take this stupid rat away and teach him how to confess."

Security men dragged him out… and away. Days and nights passed agonizingly slowly. Oscar was first set upon by specially trained dogs, leaving him no respite until his hands and legs were bleeding profusely. Then his hands and feet were tied together behind his back, using a thick rope and he was lifted to the ceiling, his body left hanging for hours till he felt his abdominal muscles would rip apart from the pain.

Then tied securely to a chair, he was violently beaten, the blows coming in harder every time he tried to close his eyes to take a moment's respite in his exhaustion. After came the whip again, the lashing continuing until lesions covered his body, at which point heated salt water was poured onto his wounds. This whole process had lasted all of two weeks, leaving Oscar scrawny, ravaged and close to death.

One morning, the questioning officer brought Oscar again to his office. He looked at the detainee whose whole physique had changed, deep, mauve traces of torture lining his eyes. He stared at Oscar and said in a calm, apparently sympathetic, voice "Tell me, do you still insist on your denial, you fool? Listen to me carefully, I pity you and do not intend to harm you in any way. You haven't seen the worst yet. This is your last chance if you really wish to resume your normal life."

"Sir, have mercy on me, please. I swear to God again and again that I do not belong to any gang or organization; I am innocent indeed. I know nothing of what you want to know", replied Oscar, his voice faint as if coming from a deep underground crypt. The officer stood up noisily, slammed the table with his fist and shouted wildly "Why did you bring this loggerhead to me before confession? Didn't I tell you I don't want to see him before he was ready to confess his crime? Take him to the Pit!"

The guards grabbed Oscar and pushed him ahead, beating and cursing him as they propelled him forwards. They finally reached 'the Pit': two meters deep and one square meter wide, with smooth concrete walls and filled thigh-high with filthy, stinking water.

The next morning, two security guards came in and found him shivering with cold and struggling to remain standing as he attempted to grab anything he could on those smooth and slippery walls.

"Changed your mind about your confession?," asked one guard with a sardonic smile. Oscar gave him a silent, emotionless look, and struggling to resist falling, collapsed onto his knees. The other guard couldn't keep his pity towards him hidden. "More severe punishment is yet to come. You'd better confess sooner; they won't let go of you until you give them answers. I advise you to spare yourself any more agony."

Oscar replied in a pain-stricken voice, "I wish I knew what I should confess to, to lift this torture off my shoulders and have a moment's rest. This is worse than death."

"Tell them you belong to that gang and everything will be over."

"But how shall I admit something I didn't do?"

"It's useless my friend. He's a damned fool and can't see what's good for him", the first guard told his colleague carelessly.

They pulled him out of 'the Pit' and dragged him to a large hall with three tables set in the middle. Each one had leather bands on top, obviously used to fasten necks and limbs. Nearby sat electric devices from which sprouted ominous wires and surgical tools of all shapes and sizes arranged on a wooden shelf by each table.

Oscar could well see horror coming, his heart pounded furiously, suddenly realizing that what he had seen was just a picnic and the worst was yet to come. And he was right. Before he could figure out the scene in front of him, he heard heavy footsteps approaching... three strong, dour men walked in, dragging behind them a man, a poor soul who already looked half dead from torture. They didn't glance at Oscar or the two guards with him, seemingly oblivious to all except the man they had with them, whom they threw onto one table and began to secure him by his neck, his hands and his feet, using the leather straps attached to the table top. One of the three guards went up to the wooden shelf nearest to the table, examined the tools as if sizing up a suitable tool for an 'operation' he was about to perform. Having chosen one, he turned and pierced the right hand of the fastened prisoner with his tool. The feeble soul, unable to stand the excruciating pain, raised an agonizing cry from the depths of his heart and Oscar, watching from the side, began to feel faint; the world around him turned with terrifying visions and he looked to his two jailers with indescribable fear.

"They've just pulled off the man's little finger's nail. They usually start with that. Wait till they pull off his thumb nail", one jailer said. The other one continued "You're next. Pull yourself together."

Oscar simply couldn't. "Please save me! I'll confess to anything and everything you want. Let them write what they want and I'll sign the papers without reading them. I beg you, please call the officer now right now."

The guards, having heard him, rushed him out of the room and called the interrogation officer. "Sir", said one of them. "The prisoner's ready to confess. Any orders?"

"Bring him in, then, to see what information he's got," the officer ordered, elated at his triumph. Once there, the officer offered him a chair and a hot cup of tea. "I understand you wish to you admit your guilt and spare yourself further inconvenience?"

The very first sip of hot, sweet tea brought solace to Oscar, the first time since being brought to this place the feeling that he was still a human being.   "Sir", he said, "I really want to admit all my crimes. Please, I beg you, help me and remind me of what you want me to say. I feel I've lost my memory."

The officer couldn't hide his delight at what he had just heard. "Great. Now we can understand each other. I only want you to sign this paper that states you are a member of an outlawed rogue organization and then tell me where Samir is, or at least the possible places he might be hiding."

"What are you going to do to me after I sign?"

"We'll refer your case to court for trial."

"Will the torture stop?"

"Sure. Our job ends here."

"I'm ready to sign anything you put down on any paper. But believe me I don't have the slightest idea about Samir's hiding place."

"Never mind! What counts now is to sign this confession statement." The officer pushed the pre-arranged document across his desk and gave him a pen. Oscar tried to read the paper when he was chided by the officer. "Come now. Sign and don't waste our time... I didn't ask you to read it."

Oscar swiftly signed the document. The officer ordered the guards to move him to another cell, where he would be detained awaiting trial.

* * * * *

Chapter Five

The National Security Chief paid a surprise visit to Lewis, the Minister of Justice, to discuss an urgent matter with him. Lewis hated the man with such a passion that whenever his name came up in conversations with his close friends, he always called him "The Despicable."

To everybody else he was known as "The Chief." He was a perfect timeserver. Words like ethics, morals, mercy, and honesty had no place in his lexicon. The only language he understood was that of his own selfish interests. Politicians feared him and privately held in contempt.

Lewis felt deeply irritated by his unexpected visit, yet managed to hide his true feelings and say a few welcoming words. "Welcome, Chief. What a pleasant surprise!"

"I'm sorry to come unexpectedly, Your Excellency. I hope I didn't upset your schedule, but I am here on extremely important and urgent business."

"What business?"

"It's regarding Your News magazine—that scandal sheet. We had tips from our own sources inside the magazine that the company was about to publish an immoral story along with pictures of you. Then they were going to blackmail you with other similar pictures. We managed to stop them from publishing the story and pictures. Our men have already raided their offices and seized all documents, including evidence and pictures that may be related to your noble self."

"What do you mean?" Lewis replied angrily. "You know damn well I have a perfectly clean personal history. If there are people who are going to spread malicious rumors and fabricated pictures for dirty money, I'll make them pay dearly."

"I'm really sorry, sir. But our photo experts have proved they were genuine pictures and I have them here in my briefcase."

"Show me," Lewis demanded.

The Chief took a photo from his case and handed it to the Minister, whose face reddened with embarrassment as soon as he saw it. The shock left him speechless. After a few minutes, he asked, "What should I do to get hold of these photos and the negatives?"

"I can give you the photos now, but I can't give you the negatives. They are held by David in a safe place your opponents cannot reach."

"Did David know about the photos?"

"Sir, to be honest, yes! He sent me to you to give you his assurance that nobody will be able to blackmail or threaten you as long as he is on your side. He expects you to be on his side in the coming few days."

"Please convey my compliments and my personal loyalty to him."

* * * * *

The days passed slowly and painfully for Angela, her son's words not leaving her thoughts, "I don't want to die, mama. I want to go out and play with my friends." Those words echoed loudly in her confused mind and depressed heart. Each time she recalled her encounter with her brother, her sorrow would deepen to depths she could not imagine. The more helpless she felt, however, the more fiercely her heart burned. Since the tragic loss of her only son, she felt a raging desire to write to her brother, to tell

62

him how insolent and arrogant he had been. She thought it might alleviate her suffering and help her regain some dignity. Eventually, she courageously sat with pen in hand, a sheet of white paper and wrote:

Dear Brian,

After a long and painful period of hesitating, I couldn't help putting these words to paper after I remembered your harsh attitude. The condescending and arrogant way you looked at me. Your bitter words and spiteful behavior which only served to add insult to injury. I hope this letter will lift some of the heavy burden off of my mind and heart.

How cruel you were when I met you after all those years! My state, physically and mentally, did not allow me to reproach you. I was overburdened with pain, exhaustion and distress. You were so proud that you wouldn't even let me call you 'brother'. You've destroyed all hope I had of finding an affectionate heart and soul. The one person I turned to for help. I hoped my brother would help to save the life of his nephew — my only child.

I didn't need anything from you but a handful of money to save my own child, only knocking on your door after all other doors had closed. I felt suffocated with despair and thought those long years of separation might have made you more caring and understanding. Pity that those years have only made you more cruel, selfish and heartless. I wish I hadn't come to you. I wish I weren't your sister.

Barry is gone. My little baby is no more. You contributed to his death with your selfishness and arrogance. He loved you and wished to see you for I told him so much about you.

Finally, I hope you will come to your senses and free yourself of your delusion one day. I hope some day you will look for the heart inside you.

Angela

Brian received the letter by post on one of the saddest and most distressful periods of his life. He had just received an official letter from the court informing him that divorce procedures had been finalized to terminate the marriage with his wife, Agnes. Now came the letter from his sister Angela to make his life all the more miserable. He hardly finished reading it when the whole world instantly darkened around him leaving him feeling shocked, his heart pounding. Suddenly he had a huge feeling of regret. Overcome with a heavy burden of deep guilt and remorse, bitter tears started to flow steadily down his face and into his chest.

The sound of his sobbing was loud in the air, sobs he had managed to suppress in the past whenever he wanted. It was now time he relieved himself of regret, remorse, guilt, and tears he told himself. Whenever he felt he was becoming weak and about to be lenient or sympathetic, he used to tell himself harshly, "Don't get weak. You are a grand personality of the state. You are a difficult equation to be reckoned with in this country. If you were caring and soft-hearted, you would never fulfill your ambition, please your superiors or satisfy your desires."

This time, though, it was different. His head fell into his open hands and he wept. "You evil soul, let go of me and my past. I am a human being. I still have a heart — a living, pulsing and caring heart. I still have feelings and emotions. I am not dead. Enough of this pretense and these illusions. Enough!" He broke into a fit of sobs.

Brian's secretary entered his office and was astonished to find him in such misery. She stood there staring at him in shock and disbelief. It was the first time she had seen him crying. Embarrassed and hesitant, she eventually managed to ask, "Are you alright, sir?"

"Oh, yes! Yes, I am."

"It's the first time since I started working here that I have seen you cry, sir."

His words came out with a sad and feeble voice, "Why shouldn't I? I've killed my nephew!"

She gulped in amazement and, putting her hand on her mouth, she asked, "What did you say?"

"Do you remember that poor woman who came here on the same day the Minister visited us? You said she looked like me?"

"Yes, I do remember her quite well. I felt so sorry for her. I have never seen such a miserable woman in my life."

"That woman is my only sister. My younger sister. She came to me to get help to treat her ailing child. I dismissed her pleas and kicked her out. I was truly an evil beast."

He paused a little and continued. "I didn't want anybody to know about her. I left my family a long time ago and hadn't seen any of them until the day my sister came to ask for help. I acted vile when I refused to listen to her. Then again when I ordered her out and when I told her to never to come back here. Her only son died later that day and I had a hand in his death."

He covered his face again to hide the ceaseless flow of tears.

"Take it easy, sir!" she said trying to ease his mind. "It's relieving to see one's mistake or guilt. You still have a chance to put things right."

He raised his head and eagerly asked, "How?"

"Go to her and apologize. She's your younger sister and will feel your regret. She badly needs someone to comfort her now."

"Do you think she'll ever forgive me? It was her only son who died! Will she forgive what I did? How I told her off for not being afraid to come to me here? How I warned her ruthlessly to not even think of ever coming back again?"

"Yes, sir, I think so. She's a woman and women, you know, are more emotional by nature. Soft words work miracles with a woman's heart."

"Thank you. Thank you."

Without delay he left his office. Getting in his car, he started the journey back to the little alley were he had been brought up. Back to where he had spent his childhood. The place he left over twenty years ago with the intention of never returning.

* * * * *

The telephone ringing loudly in the early hours awoke David. He turned nervously to turn on his bedside lamp and looked at the clock. It was nearly three.

"Hello, who is it?"

"I'm extremely sorry to wake you up at this time, sir," an aide said. "But I have to tell you that Jack has been arrested and the drugs with him have been seized."

David sat up in bed and cried, "What?! Who's the idiot who searched my private plane?

"The lawyer called to tell me that Jack is being detained at Customs. He said that a new Customs officer ordered the seizure of the drugs and took Jack into custody for questioning."

"The little bugger will pay dearly for this."

"Your orders, sir?"

"Leave it to me to handle."

He went to the hall downstairs, lit a cigar and asked the maid to make him a cup of coffee. He sat there gazing at the smoke circles from his cigar and thinking this sudden problem over, looking now and then at the pendulum clock on the opposite wall. He picked up the receiver and called the National Security Chief. It took a long time till the sleepy Chief eventually answered.

"Hello!"

"David here, Chief. I know it's an awkward time to call, but the matter is urgent and can't wait."

"It's OK, David. What is it?"

"A stupid Customs officer insisted on searching my private plane and seized the pilot with some drugs."

"There must be a mistake. All Customs officers have been provided with clear and strict instructions. They know they should never inspect your plane. You said it was carrying some drugs?"

"Shall I take this question as an interrogation?"

"Certainly not. I'm sorry if I failed to use the right expression. But it's better for both of us if I know the nature of the consignment. It's up to you, sir, whether you want to tell me or not."

"It's not a secret. They were spirit drugs. You know what I mean."

"Oh, yes. Now I know. Don't worry. I'll handle it."

"I shall not go back to bed until the pilot and the drugs are released. Is that clear?!"

"Don't worry about it, David. Consider it done."

"I also want you to discipline that haughty-headed Customs officer and make an example of him. No other officer should ever dare to make the same mistake."

"Understood, sir."

The Chief called the Customs General Director at once and ordered the immediate release of the pilot and drugs and indicated that all relevant documents be destroyed. He also ordered the officer involved to be sent back to his commanding section and immediately to his office.

The customs officer arrived at the Chief's office where he was told to wait till he arrived. He was obviously in an awkward position and had no idea why he had been called to the Security Chief's office. "I bet it has something to do with the drugs I seized at the airport. Maybe he has some questions about it, or perhaps he wants to thank me for doing my job," the officer thought to himself.

A long, boring and nerve-racking hour passed before the private secretary finally told him the Chief wanted him to come in. He knocked at the door and heard a loud voice come through the loudspeaker:

"Come in. Quiet."

The officer opened the door and looked amazed at the huge office with a meeting table for at least twenty people. Flat TV screens were all over the walls and a spacious library was crammed full of books, audio-and video-cassettes and CDs. He walked a few steps in when he suddenly heard alarm sirens. Puzzled, he paused for a second and then heard a voice begin to give him instructions.

"Stop. Step back. Walk. Don't walk. Move forward!"

With confused, hesitant steps, he moved toward the Chief who was watching a cowboy movie on one of the wide screens on the left-side wall.

"Good morning, sir."

The Chief didn't return the greeting. After a short while of dead silence, he told the officer to sit down. Meanwhile, the Chief still kept his eyes glued to the screen.

"I have only a couple of words to tell you and I've no time to waste."

"Yes, sir. I am all ears."

"You are a low-ranking officer and you still have a long way to go. This state has its men who run the affairs and set the laws."

"Pardon me, sir. I didn't get what you said."

"What you did yesterday is unacceptable in our system. Your seizure of the drugs was a mistake. Many people need these drugs. Do you want to kill them?!"

"But, sir, the drugs were not medicine as the pilot claimed. Lab tests showed it was pure heroin. I didn't act on my own; I was only doing my duty and enforcing the law."

"What law? When I say drugs I mean legal drugs, you fool."

The officer nodded sadly.

"Now I understand, sir."

"I'll give you a chance and I won't punish you this time. Go back to work and don't act off your head again. Be careful when you deal with the wealthy from now on. You can gain lots of benefits in your current position. Many young people envy you for it."

"Yes, sir. Thank you."

* * * * *

Chapter Six

Decorations filled the streets, with every building and shop windows in the entire Capital, bright colored lights scattered throughout all the roads and covered rooftops of every building and shop window in the entire Capital, turning the city into a thing of beauty, shining like a bride on her wedding day. A huge glittering star filled with lights lit the city like a shining sun even at nighttime, illuminating the parties and bandstands spread all over. The air was filled with joyful music and the delightful sounds and colors of the breathtaking fireworks, the night sky infused with ever changing dazzling designs in all shapes and sizes. The Capital was celebrating an annual event, the Leader's Birthday. Participation was compulsory if one wished to spare oneself the serious accusation of treason and siding with the 'enemies of the nation'. This year the grand party was held at the Palace of Fantasy, this 'happy' occasion transmitted live worldwide via the official radio and TV channels.

The party was attended by all government ministers, officials, all notables and leading businessmen in addition to a select number of famous writers, journalists, poets and artists.

The celebrations were also, of course, watched by the lamenting poor sectors of society who, with a determination yet also with silence, objected to so much being spent so lavishly on such an individual occasion with so many resources being brought in and used with disregard to the plight of the majority of the population.

Marilyn, quick to seize the opportunity to attract attention to her personal as well as her public qualities, delivered a short and emotional speech, "Personally and on behalf of the dignitaries, businessmen and celebrities sharing with us this joyful occasion, I would like to extend the most sincere congratulations to our Leader, and wishes for a long, fruitful and healthy life and eternal happiness."

Her audience looked on startled – it was not conventional for the Leader's wife to extend congratulations on behalf of the Cabinet as well as the notables on such an occasion. The Leader suppressed his anger, looking at her with obvious astonishment. He didn't utter a single word; rather pretending approval of what she had done, he thanked her openly for her gesture.

Upon returning to their Presidential Palace, the Leader kept nervously silent; he naturally didn't approve of her conduct at the party, but at the same time he didn't want to stir up the hornet's nest inside her. Suddenly, she broke the heavy silence.

"You were just great at your Birthday Party today, dear. You were really brilliant and shining... but you seem a bit preoccupied. I hope I'm the one who engages your mind so much!"

"Very kind of you, Marilyn, thank you! But I wish from the bottom of my heart you hadn't caused me such public embarrassment once again."

"What? Is this my reward? I thought you were going to thank me for publicly announcing my love and devotion to you. I don't know why you can't stand anymore what I say! You're becoming too sensitive. You've changed."

"You very well know, Marilyn, there were Cabinet ministers and top-ranking officials attending. It wasn't diplomatic of you to speak on their behalf," he replied calmly.

"What diplomacy you're talking about? Have you forgotten I am the First Lady... and will be Prime Minister soon, whether those ministers and officials like it or not. I also wanted to prepare the ground for my future addresses."

He swallowed his anger again, preferring to keep his mouth shut; the hornets weren't raging yet so it was wiser just to leave it at that. As luck would have it, he turned to see the butler walk in carrying the telephone, telling him Lewis was on the line. He took the receiver, irritated that somebody would call at such a late hour, especially since the Minister of Justice had been physically there at the party.

"Yes, Lewis. What is it?," he asked with apparent serenity.

"I'm extremely sorry to disturb you, Mr. President. But the matter is so urgent that it can't be postponed. Michael's condition deteriorated suddenly and seriously this evening... he's now dying. The chief doctor at the hospital called me to inform you that Michael wishes to see us as soon as possible. I've already informed Danny and Tony and the three of us are on our way right now to see him."

"Alright. I'll leave at once."

He handed the receiver back to the waiting butler, looked grimly at his wife and said,

"I have to rush to the hospital. Lewis has just told me Michael is dying and wants to see me."

"I'll go with you to see him."

"You don't need to, dear. It's late and I'll convey your sincere wishes to him."

She walked with him to the front door struggling to hide her joy at the news she had so eagerly been awaiting. It was no secret she didn't like Michael, yet she had to feign respect for him so as not to offend George, for she knew quite well the extent of his influence upon her husband.

The Leader went straight to Michael's ward to see his three brothers already sitting in solemn silence at Michael's side. The Leader greeted him warmly.

"How do you feel Michael?"

With a feeble voice that could hardly be heard, came the reply,

"As you see, illness has taken a heavy toll on me. I'm afraid I won't recover this time."

"Don't say that. I gave my orders to all doctors in the hospital to keep constant vigilance and dedicate all efforts to provide the best treatment for you. You'll get well soon."

"No, no. I don't think so. I'm not so optimistic, brother. That's why I wanted you all to meet here, to bid you all farewell and to give you some pieces of advice before I depart this life, this journey of illusion I had made until now. I am your eldest brother and that's my duty towards you all and what my conscience tells me to do."

"Don't talk like this. The doctors here are capable of curing your illnes. It's only a matter of days and you'll leave this hospital in perfect health", replied the Leader.

Gulping back his tears, Lewis said, "We'd like to see you strong, so don't give up hope."

Danny was the next to speak,

"We'll try our hardest to help you recover soon and see you among us. We need you here, we need your wisdom."

Michael scanned their faces and stretched out a hand, "Give me a hand. Support me!"

Danny and Tony hurried to raise him up slowly from the bed whilst Lewis fluffed up some pillows behind his back to help him sit up. He gave them a solemn look.

"Lend me all your ears, Keep your hands always joined together in one single unshakeable grip. Support each other and never let anyone drive a wedge between you."

He then asked them to leave him alone with George.

"Listen to me carefully, George. Your absolute power has no precedence in history. You are the Leader of the most powerful state ever on this planet. Remember that death is an undeniable fact of life - nobody lives forever. Therefore, do your best to rid the state of injustice for it is the worst of all evils. I ask you to help the poor and the deprived, they've suffered a great deal under previous rules and they have not been much better off under my government either.

"I warn you against the unsatisfiable lusts of greed, of dealings and usury and dealing with those whose only love in life is to pile up more and more wealth out of dishonest profits. Their selfishness knows no bounds and worst of all, they neither wish nor do good to anybody. Bring honest and sincere people closer to you and make them your trusted confidants.

"One last word, George. Beware the intrigues of your wife and her parents. Your brothers are your right hand; help them and support them to help you."

"Thank you, Michael, for your invaluable advice. But why are you warning me to beware of my wife?"

"Marilyn, I believe, is an ambitious, selfish and self-centered woman valuing nothing but herself. She doesn't hold any respect or appreciation for you. This certainly weakens you personally and undermines your authority. She is a wily and dangerous woman and she is exploiting your kind and noble heart.

"A wife of this sort will never make life easier for anybody, particularly you, unless she gets what she wants, and, even if she gets what she wants. Open your eyes wide, George, and don't be so gullible as to let her trick you by her honeyed words. She's only using you as a ladder to climb to the top."

George was left extremely annoyed by Michael's words yet his face showed only understanding and appreciation. He thanked Michael, kissed him good-bye and left, muttering to himself, "Poor Michael, he no longer realizes what he is saying."

The meeting was held at Julian's grandfather's house and drew together Samir with a number of his colleagues, all journalists who opposed the totalitarian system of the government they saw was in place. It was an old, almost derelict house, and Julian, a member of Samir's group, had kept the keys safe since the passing of his grandfather. Besides, it was also his hiding place away from the scrutiny of security watchdogs.

Samir opened the meeting with a few words of welcome, thanking the members for coming.

"Dear Comrades! Injustice is everywhere in our country, corruption has spread to peak levels, taxes are already sky-high, shopkeepers and market dealers are pursuing crafty methods to fleece as much money as they can out of people's pockets. Moral corruption has reached scandalous levels, our society is now preoccupied only with loose, pointless and too often sordid serials on the TV and radio as well as in magazine articles and pictures. This ethical deterioration has become the public culture of our society.

"Do I need to remind you of the poor and the starving? The great majority of our people are living below the poverty line. Our fellow citizens have been turned into mere slaves serving the wealthy, whose influential class dominates financial institutions and international bodies controlling every means of life. The situation is very grim and the prospects look even grimmer. The poor are now paying the price for the well-being of the ever greedy rich. With the gap between the two classes rapidly widening, the stupid rich don't even realize that they will never be safe as long as they are surrounded by the vast majority of the deprived classes they so harshly exploit, monopolizing political power as well as all financial, industrial and commercial assets.

"Their ethical standards have reached rock bottom. They now sell expired medicines and promote useless ones. You may have also heard the tragic story of the poor child, Barry, who lost his life when he took a rotten, out-of-date medicine his parents had struggled so hard to raise money to buy in hopes of easing his suffering. The medicine was purchased from a pharmacy owned by a rich family; the hospital he had been rushed to refused to admit the dying child until his outrageously high treatment cost, which they could not afford, was paid. Such misfortune, I believe, can be seen repeated everyday, and for families across the whole country, even though official statistics do not exist.

"You may also have heard about the brutality with which my own house was set upon and my wife and little children terrorized. The assault squad searched every inch in my house turning the whole place upside down and confiscating everything they could lay their hands on for any clue. When they finished they rushed to my cousin Oscar's house where they practiced the same brutality before they took away poor, peaceful, good-natured Oscar who's only crime was that he is my cousin. He was humiliated and beaten in front of his wife and children before he was arrested and taken to the State Security Directorate where he was ruthlessly tortured for days, and in all that time he was allowed no visitors due to 'security reasons'. God only knows his whereabouts now or what has become of him. Security police still raid his house every now and then to question his wife and children just to terrify them."

Neville stood up to ask,

"What are we going to do in these grim and dark conditions? Isn't there any glimpse of light at the end of the tunnel?"

"A small bunch of crooks have managed, after taking control of all the living resources, to persuade many people to accept the de facto status quo and to share with them the life of illusion they are leading. On the other hand, simple and gullible people who have got used to their way and standard of living and accepted it as their predetermined destiny, are being manipulated all the time by the official mass media. Who would have thought only a short while ago, that the authorities would bug every street corner, every marketplace, station and public facility with spy cameras, monitoring every movement of their own citizens?

"In spite of all this, we should never despair. It's only a matter of time before people become aware of the illusion they have been coerced to live under so far. To find salvation, we must first seek it," explained Samir.

John looked at his watch,

"Samir, we must leave now. It's almost midnight. You know they dispatch more security patrols after midnight. We don't want to be caught."

Samir sighed and checked the time,

"John's right. We must leave now, though cautiously … Go out one by one, and split up in different directions."

* * * * *

Michael breathed his last breath only two days after the visit from his brothers. He was just over eighty, and had been seriously ill, fighting for life for quite a while. Doctors had tried their hardest to keep him alive but to no avail.

His funeral was transmitted live on all media channels and a three-day national period of mourning was announced.

Marilyn went to see the Leader in his office purporting sadness,

"We have lost an honest and loyal patriot. His demise has touched me deeply."

"Thank you, Marilyn."

"I know it's not the right moment to remind you of my request, but I only wanted to draw your attention to it. I learned you've called the Cabinet to convene tomorrow in an emergency meeting now that the official mourning is over."

"That's right. Michael's successor must be named."

"And who's that person going to be?", she asked coquettishly. "I hope I will be that successor!"

"I'll leave it a surprise for everyone," he replied with a smile.

A cunning, ambitious lady, she clearly understood he meant her by his "surprise", but she remained doubtful. As long as an official decision in this respect has not been taken and announced, all possibilities remain on the table and doors of doubt remained open.

The next day, she smoked nervously and consumed many cups of coffee, impatiently waiting for the outcome of that cabinet meeting.

With an unsteady hand, she picked up the receiver and called her mother in a worried tone.

"Hello, Mother. How are you?"

"Hello, Marilyn. We're alright. Any news?"

"I don't know why I am becoming so uneasy and anxious! George is now meeting with the Cabinet to choose Michael's successor. I'm really afraid they won't name me for the post. All my dreams and plans would be broken. It would be an unbearable nightmare. My only rival is Lewis and he hates me with a vengeance."

"Don't worry, Marilyn. Your father has already dealt with him and coerced him into keeping quiet. But tell me, how was George's mood when he left this morning?"

"Normal. He tried to set my mind at rest and made an encouraging promise, though he wanted to leave the decision as a surprise, he said."

"Oh, that's another good sign. So, don't worry, dear. Things will go your way."

At that moment, from her window Marilyn noticed George's car coming in through the gate.

"Is he back then? Ok, I'm waiting for your call soon, my dear, to hear the good news. Good-bye for now," her mother said in a hopeful tone.

And good news it was all right. George tried hard to hide his true feelings when he talked to her, smiling,

"I made the Cabinet grant you your request. I've kept my promise and fulfilled your dream for you, darling. I congratulate you from the bottom of my heart."

She jumped for joy and hugged him,

"Thank you so much, George, for your trust. I really appreciate it. Today, I am the happiest woman on earth. I'll work hard to prove I deserve your trust. Oh, George. You've proven to me that you truly do love me."

"You know, I'm always keen to make you happy and fulfill your desires."

"Tell me, how did the meeting go? How did the ministers take it? Did any one raise a word of caution or objection?"

"Who dares? Nobody had any reservations against my decision, of course. They all approved with obvious satisfaction."

"Thank you, George. What did Lewis think? He had a burning ambition for quite a while to succeed Michael, I reckon."

"You know he was the favourite candidate. He's my brother and he indeed had an eye on the post, but he would not dare object to my decisions."

"I hope he won't stir up trouble for me in my new job."

"No, no. I definitely don't think so. Forget about him now. Let's discuss the arrangements for the grand celebrations for this happy occasion. The grandest in history."

"Thank you, my dearest George. I'll never forget this favour."

Marilyn asked the housemaid to bring them champagne so she could   toast to her now secured, post.

* * * * *

Maurice was suddenly filled with horror and he felt his heart jump almost jump out of his chest. He thought his hiding box had been discovered and that he would be caught within minutes and he held his breath as tight as he could. Yet, he couldn't help thinking of his mother and father and the fate he was going to face if that officer did find him; the money he had borrowed to give to the driver to smuggle him out of the country would be lost, the kind-hearted truck driver who he had paid to take him to the "Republic of Illusion" would be charged with "smuggling illegal immigrants" and would be severely punished. The dream of starting a new life in a new country would be completely destroyed forever, leaving him helpless and unable to help his father out of prison or stand on his own feet again... great expectations would come to a tragic end.

* ** **

The truck driver tried hard to keep his composure while he moved to carry out the officer's order to open the truck box where Maurice was hiding. He was driving the key into the lock, his hand trembling, when he heard the Customs Director telling the inspection officer to quickly finish checking the truck as the ferry was now ready for inspection before setting out to sea.

"Yes, sir. Just finished."

The officer gave the truck papers back to the driver and told him to hurry up to catch the boat.

With a deep sigh of relief by both the driver and Maurice, the driver rushed into the ferry. Once the ferry's draw-bridge gate closed right behind them, they were off into a rough sea. Huge, high waves rocked the ship up-and-down and from side-to-side during the entire three-hour crossing. Maurice's maiden voyage by sea brought on heavy sea-sickness and he couldn't stop himself from bringing up everything in his stomach onto his clothes and suitcase as he crouched in that grave-like truck box. The nauseating voyage in that tiny box passed so slowly that he thought it would never end, and by the time the rocking stopped and the ferry dropped anchor at the destination, Maurice was in an appalling condition, gasping for air as the appalling stench of his retching filled the tightly closed place.

What lessened his suffering was the sight of his mother's silent farewell and tearful eyes, and his little sister's innocent face. He also remembered his father who was waiting for him to get him out of prison. From now on, he thought, things will can only get better, time will pass rapidly, and life will become easier in the land of illusion where he will achieve his goals and fulfill his dreams. He had seen his relatives and friends coming back from this country with luxury cars, the latest technologies, fortunes with which they built modern and spacious houses and villas in his village. He had also seen the big-hearted welcome the returning expatriates had received in his village.

The truck rushed to the highway as soon as it got through customs procedures. The driver pulled up at a convenient roadside parking area and, to Maurice's great relief, he opened the truck box and helped him move out of it. He couldn't stand on his feet quite yet, having excruciating cramp in his legs from being cooped up for so long, and it took him some time, with the patient driver's help, before he could move his body and walk a few steps with the patient driver's help. The kindhearted driver gave him some water to clean his clothes and a bottle of fresh water to drink.

"We're here at last. My job is over now and I must leave you right away before the police discover our adventure."

"Thank you so much, you've been very kind. Please tell my mother I'm OK when you go back."

"Sure I will, don't worry, I haven't forgotten that part of the deal. Goodbye and God bless."

The truck flew off leaving Maurice on his own. He looked around feeling absolutely lost and confused, not knowing where he was or which direction to go. He took out a slip of paper a friend had given him from his pocket and read the telephone number to call once he arrived in the "Republic of Illusion." Maurice took the coloured lights he could see from a distance as a guide to reach a main street bustling with city life, many people rushing in all directions, shop windows filled with objects of all shapes and colours, huge ad signs and screens. He was filled with awe and   paused to take in some of his surroundings. It was a sharp contrast to what he used to seeing in his simple, little village. City women were barely dressed, with tight, manly shirts and "pants", and men dressed almost effeminate from their hairstyles to their court shoes and boots.

He suddenly realised that nobody around him had even noticed his presence or was even bothered - another sharp contrast to the scenes in the narrow, intimate streets of his village where people are keen to greet each other warmly, often with kisses. In the city, rushing was the name of the game, rushing to catch a taxi, bus or train; rushing to get somewhere; or even rushing to buy or pick up something from the shops before closing time; rushing to do everything due to the time-consuming nature of city life.

He stopped comparing and analysing. He was exhausted and decided to call his friend Benedict who would put him up in his flat until he found work and was able to rent a place of his own.

"Hello. Who is it?", came Benedict's sleepy voice.

"I'm sorry to call at this late hour, but I've just arrived in the Republic of Illusion and need to talk to you. Do you remember me, Benedict?"

"Your voice is familiar."

"I am your friend Maurice Tailor."

"Oh, yes. Hello Maurice. How are you? Where are you calling from?"

"Near a big train station."

"There's a number of big stations in this city. Which one is it?"

"I don't know. I can't read the language."

"All right. Stop a taxi and sign to the driver you're going to call me and ask him to talk to me. I'll tell him the way to my address."

In about half an hour the two friends were hugging each other warmly at Benedict's front door. They hadn't met for over five years, ever since Benedict had left the village when he was twenty on his way to the "Republic of Illusion". It was here that he had sought political asylum because of his political opposition to the authorities back home and his staunch demands for reform as a university student. He was known among his colleagues and friends as a handsome, good-mannered and intelligent chap. As an activist, he was respected and admired by all his fellow villagers.

Maurice stepped back and exclaimed,

"You've changed a lot, Benedict! You look double your age!"

Benedict invited him in to explain,

"It's the life here my friend. Time passes so quickly and working in a big city like this consumes up your energy and adds years to your age. It's a tough and empty life here. Everybody is preoccupied with their own concerns and problems, of which there are no shortage, rushing around seeking lost, and sadly unattainable happiness. Everyone who joins in will have to be in the same illusive boat."

"This is frightening, Benedict."

"Sorry, Maurice. I didn't mean to frighten you. I am only trying to show you the right and true picture of life in the "Republic of Illusion," and to explain why I look double my age. If you had asked me, I would've advised you not to come."

"Is life so miserable and difficult in this country? I tell you frankly, I didn't come here because I wanted to or because I thought I would like it here. But because of the difficult situation back home, you know, that's what forced me to come."

"I didn't exactly mean it's so miserable here, it may well be easy and comfortable. But the price one has to pay to live and work in this country is extremely high."

"Yet, Benedict, even life in our own country has tremendously changed. Many people there lead a miserable, materialistic life now. They compete fiercely with each other through dishonest means in a daily struggle of materialistic pettiness."

"I fully agree with you. People who struggle to change the eternal universal rules and totally ignore the spiritual and moral aspects of competition will end up paying themselves, as well as making others, including their own children, pay dearly in the future for their misconceptions, no matter how comfortable and luxurious their current life may be."

Maurice felt free to look around the sitting room. He saw four lavish leather sofas, a large flat screenTV screen TV with state of the art video equipment, as well as a modern computer with full accessories. Admiring the honey-brown wooden floor, he said,

"What a beautiful house you have, Benedict. You're living in a palace. By the way, I must also add, it's a beautiful city."

"Yes, it is in fact. There are more decorations up these days to celebrate the Leader George's birthday."

" I'm eager to see everything."

" You will soon, Maurice. Now tell me about our village and the folks back home. I miss it; I miss my friends, the narrow lanes, the trees, the green grass, the fresh air, the bright sun. I miss it all."

"The village hasn't changed a bit, it's still the very same place you left it. All your friends are alright. Some got married, some have left for nearby cities and towns for work. But all the neighbouring villages have changed a lot. Most fertile land has been converted to high-rise buildings and guarded housing units. Giant multi-national companies run such big projects. Most farmers were persuaded to sell their land to these powerful corporations."

"By the way, how's our friend Luke?"

"He's doing really good. The heavens have been generous to him; he now owns a big farm where most villagers work."

"Is he still a simple and good man or has he changed?" Benedict asked.

"He's the only one who has not been spoiled by his enormous wealth. He still goes to church every Sunday and gives generously to local charities and the needy."

"What a strange and ironic destiny! You know, he intended to come here with me in the same truck that brought me into this country. It was the sudden death of his grandfather that prevented him from leaving the village and made him change his mind at the last minute about ever going abroad."

"I didn't know that. Maybe, as you said Heaven has chosen a much better destiny for his future!"

"And you told me his good fortune hasn't changed him as it has done to many other people."

Benedict suddenly looked at his watch,

"Wow. It's already two in the morning... you must have some rest, you look awfully tired. Tomorrow we'll go on a tour of the city. You're lucky I'm off work for a couple of days."

* * * * *

Brian arrived at his old alley to find himself surrounded by an astonished crowd. It was the first time ever they had seen such a big and high-class car in their quarter. Children circled the car in cheerful, yet amazed circles which reminded Brian of those good old days when he did the same each time he saw a car, any car, come down the alley.

The crowds prevented him from driving further so he parked, got out of the car and began the short walk up to his old home. Memories, some sweet and some bitter, filled his mind—he remembered his walks along these narrow dirty alleys; he remembered his playful childhood and teenage years in this quarter; he remembered his parents who died , still unhappy over his obstinate rebellion. His memories brought him up to the day he had left the quarter, his father shouting at him as he left the house, cursing the day he had been born whilst and his mother begged 'dad' to forgive him, holding onto him with all her strength as she pleaded with him to stay.

Bitter tears of remorse ran down his face, almost hidden behind wide dark glasses. Somehow he managed to fight back his tears as he walked into a small shop near his old house. An aged, wrinkly-faced man sat behind an old wooden bar, a man Brian recognised from long ago. He pointed at an almost crumbling, apparently neglected house, opposite the shop,

"Do you know a woman called Angela Lamp who lived there with her family?"

"Yes, I know her very well. But she left since she got married."

"Do you know where she lives now?"

"Yes, I went to give my condolences to her husband Adam yesterday. Their only son died of a serious illness a couple of days ago. Everybody knew their story and talked about it. It was in the newspapers. The mother is so grieved at the tragic loss of her child—poor soul."

"Can you show me how to go to her new address?" Brian asked.

"It's not far. You didn't tell me who you are, sir," the shopkeeper replied.

"I am a relative of hers. I came to be close to her in her grief."

"I'll send my son with you to her house."

The old shopkeeper called out to his son Sammy to help Brian find Angela's new address. They stopped at a small, humble building in a poor quarter. The boy pointed to the building.

"There, sir. That's the house."

Brian gave the boy small coin to thank him. He walked to the front door and stood there, hesitant to knock, struggling to overcome his pride.

Adam opened the door to face a strange gentleman wearing a black suit, a red tie, a clean white shirt, covering his eyes with wide dark glasses and apparently looking like a very rich man. Adam grew suspicious of the person he was facing. He didn't know Brian and Brian didn't know him either.

"Yes, sir. Can I help you?"

"Are you Adam?" Brian asked very politely.

"Yes. But I didn't have the honor to meet you before, sir," Adam replied, still puzzled.

"I'm Brian – Angela's brother."

Adam couldn't believe what he had heard. Unconsciously, he began to repeat, "Brian?, Brian?" and could utter no more words. Brian took the glasses off his red and swollen eyes and continued in a sad, repentant voice,

"Yes, I am Brian. I'd like to see my sister, please!"

"Come in. I'll tell her you're here"

He went to Angela and whispered in her ear, still not believing his eyes,

"You'll not believe what I'll tell you... your brother Brian is here in the sitting room. He came to see you. What should I tell him?"

Her eyes widened with fury and amazement.

"What? Brian? Why is he here? What does that contemptuous boy want from me now? Why did he come? Barry's dead. I don't want to see him here... throw him out of my house like he threw me out of his office."

Adam put his hand on her mouth.

"Keep your voice down, he can hear you... No, Angela, no. It's not right; not you; not us. We shouldn't make the same mistake he had made."

"But I don't even want to see his face ... I hate him ... he had a hand in killing my son... he insulted me and threw me out of his office."

"Angela. Angela, dear. You should give him a chance, he might've come to apologize. Listen first to what he wants to say before you judge him. Please, for my sake, see him. Our son's passed away now. It's the will of the Almighty."

She gave him a feeble look and reluctantly succumbed to his request.

"Alright, I'll see him, but only for your sake. Let him in and let's see what that big-head wants to say".

Brian waited anxiously in the poorly furnished sitting room where there was only one old second-hand sofa and a shabby old rug hardly covering half the room. He wondered, "Will she throw me out as I did to her in my office? Will she accept my apology? What shall I say?"

He suddenly heard Adam inviting him in. He stood up and hesitantly walked toward her room.

She sat up in bed the moment her eyes met his. There, was her brother who had always disobeyed his parents, who left her on her own when she was a child over two decades ago, who had kicked her out of his office when she came to him asking for help... standing before her humbly asking her pardon.

Distressing thoughts passed quickly through her mind as she aimed her venomous gaze at him. He looked at her remorsefully and neither of them said a word.

Slowly, with heavy steps, he walked to her bed, bowed to kiss her hands as repentant tears fell on them.

"Forgive me, Angela. What I did to you and your son was a crime. I admit that and I've come to apologize. I've had it on my conscience for a long time. Your letter opened my eyes... and my heart. You've got me out of my illusions. Please, please forgive me, dear sister!"

Now she looked at him with a mixture of blame and sympathy, attempting hard to suppress her emotions, managing somehow to remain silent. Brian carried on,

"Please accept my apology. I've returned to abide by the commandments of my Creator. I'll go and apologize to Barry in his grave."

Barry's name suddenly sparked a flow of hot tears and a fit of burning sobs. Her tongue went heavy,

"Why did you do it, Brian?"

Before he uttered an answer, Adam intervened.

"It's your brother, Angela. He's here to apologize and show his repentance. Our son's death is God's will. There's no need to lay the blame on anybody now."

With a brotherly kiss on her forehead and remorseful tears on his cheeks, Brian made an emotional confession.

"I've got my just punishment, Angela. I never knew happiness since I left home. I wish I hadn't been so rebellious. The memory of our father shouting as he threw me out of the house constantly shadowed me, even in sleep, giving me terrible nightmares. I tried to forget by drinking heavily, by going to noisy parties, by staying up late at night, but it was all in vain. Weeks and months only added to my sadness and misery.

"Yet people envied me for my plight thinking I was happy. They couldn't see the truth. Angela, I am pleading with you to forgive me, I've had enough of misery and anguish. My eldest son Bill left me when I needed him most after years of constant arguing. He was as rebellious as I had been with my parents. My wife Agnes divorced me after all I did for her, never showing any appreciation or understanding. She used to insult me, always reminding me that I was no more than 'a street boy'. She took Sally, our daughter with her and forbade me from seeing her. Angela, please, I can't stand it any longer."

Angela felt that she also could not stand the impact of his pleading. She could feel that he was genuine this time, that he was sincere in his repentance. She slowly got up from her bed, hugged him tightly and they both wept together,

"Thank Heaven! The tragedy of my son's passing has brought life into my brother's heart."

Chapter Seven

Once the Titanic Spacecraft was finally assembled, the Defense Minister, on orders from the Leader gave instructions to the project engineers to start testing. The Leader was present along with a number of army top brass and Cabinet ministers, all wearing heavy duty ear plugs.

The craft's enormous engines roared to life, the noise reverberating all around the city. People suspected enemy jet fighters were raiding their Capital as the ear-splitting din shattered the windows of houses near the base, sending small shards of glass flying everywhere. Frightened men, women and children ran in the streets to find out what was happening, scanning the skies in the direction where the thunderous noise seemed to come. The coarse voice of the official announcer broke the confusion. All eyes turned to the giant TV screens.

"We congratulate our great people on this immense success and this marvelous technological advancement. With extraordinary success the "Fantasy Craft", finally complete and fully assembled, has been tested at the great military base specifically prepared for this purpose. This craft possesses mighty capabilities made possible by utilizing the most advanced technology ever produced by humankind. Our noble Leader will shortly speak to his people on this grand occasion."

People everywhere, following the pictures on the official TV, baffled at the sight of the huge spacecraft moving magnificently before their eyes.

"It's enormous!"

"It's a modern wonder greater than the Seven Wonders of the World!"

"Why is it so vast? What is it for?"

The live transmission was interrupted by a loud fanfare to introduce the Leader's speech.

"My great people. This is a momentous day. This is the day of our colossal scientific triumph. Here you see with your own eyes the spacecraft, and hear its powerful engines roaring. It is an historical achievement. A remarkable accomplishment in human history, without peer. We have spent lavishly on this undertaking and we are very proud of the results. This craft will provide us security against any conceivable threat. With it, we will remain the most powerful striking force in history- no nation on earth has ever reached this mighty position or this technological and scientific victory. We can now boast that we are the only superpower on the face of the earth with the capability to defeat all aggressors. We are free to impose our will and expand our rule to cover the whole world."

A storm of applause shook the place, with intermittent shouts hailing the Leader and pledges of loyalty and praise heralding the steps of his triumphant march forward.

* * * * *

Sad, frightened, and perplexed, Oscar, after months in detention finally sat in a side room of the Courts Complex awaiting the trial which would decide his fate. He recalled the rumors he had heard about the injustice and cruelty some judges showed and dispensed against suspects like him. He remembered his wife and children. "What would become of them?," he wondered, "if I was sentenced to life imprisonment or even to death, what then?"

Suddenly he heard the guards ordering him to go inside the courtroom and to sit in the dock.

The Judge and his two aides entered and took their seats on the bench. An ominous silence filled the room as all eyes focused on them. The Judge read through the file before him, and then looked across to Oscar.

"Your name?... Your job? ... Your age?"

In a low voice, obviously pleading for sympathy, Oscar replied,

"My name's Oscar Plumber, Sir. I am a farmer. I'm forty years old."

"You are charged with dissidence, conspiracy against the regime, belonging to an outlawed organization and concealing valuable information about other dissidents and wanted suspects. How do you plead?"

"I know nothing about this organization and I did not plot against anybody, Sir."

"Your confession is here in front of me. There is no need for denial."

The presiding Judge then nodded at the Public Prosecutor to deliver his speech, who gave Oscar an evil leer and went on,

"I plead to the honorable board to inflict the severest punishment on the accused without pity or mercy. It has been undoubtedly confirmed by solid evidence and by his own unambiguous confession that he was actively involved in an evil conspiracy against the regime, which clearly makes him guilty of high treason—a crime, as the honorable board well knows, that deserves the harshest capital punishment. This criminal must be made an example."

The Judge turned to Oscar's defense lawyer.

"Do you have anything to say in response to the Prosecution?"

"Your Honor, I kindly ask you to give my client a minimum sentence in the light of his full confession to the charges brought against him. This is a clear indication that he is sorry for his actions. He was duped by that rogue organization into plotting against our government. I also plead to your conscience to take the difficult conditions of his family into consideration. He is, after all, their sole provider. Thank you."

The Judge turned to face Oscar and asked,

"Do you have anything to say?"

"Your Honor, I did nothing against the law. I don't understand why my lawyer, who should defend my case, has confirmed my confession of the charges against me when I have never met him and never discussed my case with him."

"Why then have you confessed if you are innocent as you claim?", the Judge replied angrily. "Of course you will reiterate the usual excuse, 'They have extracted my confession under torture.' However, I want to assure you the Prosecution has presented the court with secret indicting evidence."

"Your Honor, I swear to God I've told you the truth. They coerced me into confessing crimes I have not committed. They forced me to sign under torture they threatened to pull off the nails of my fingers and toes and the only escape from this was to sign. And I know nothing about any secret evidence."

The Judge turned back to the Public Prosecutor.

"Any comment?"

"Your Honor, these are absolute lies. You know our government is one of the very few authorities in the world known to be staunch defenders of human rights and public freedoms. We do not resort to torture of any sort. On the contrary, we oppose those who use such inhumane methods."

Oscar couldn't help himself and began to cry bitterly,

"Sir, if flogging me with whips and sticks till I fall to the ground fainting isn't torture, what is? If unleashing fierce trained dogs to bite deep into my flesh and shred off my clothing isn't torture, then what is? If tying my hands and legs firmly together behind my back and lifting me with the same chains up to the ceiling, leaving me hanging up there for hours till I felt my gut muscles burn with pain isn't torture, what is? If fastening me tight to a chair for many hours every day and punching me endlessly on my head isn't torture, what is? If kicking me to the ground tied to that chair so my body and head hit the bare, concrete floor - risking killing me each time - isn't torture, what is? If whipping me till my skin is filled with sores and then pouring salt on my open wounds isn't torture, what is? Your Honor, I may need hours to describe the methods of torture they practiced on me."

"Is what he says true?", the Judge asked the Public Prosecutor.

"Your Honor, here's a man who is an expert liar. He has not gone through any sort of torture. I request calling the first of two witnesses we have to testify in support of the charges against him."

The Judge ordered the usher to call the first witness in. After checking identity and oath formalities, he began questioning the witnesses.

"Do you know that man in the dock?"

"No, Your Honor, I don't. I only met him that day in the café."

"How did you know this man was Oscar and the man he met was Samir?"

"I had seen Samir's picture in the newspapers and read the appeal put out to anybody who knew something about him to come forward with information. My patriotic duty drove me to tell the police what I knew. When I told the officer I had seen him with another man, he showed me a number of pictures and asked me to recognize or identify those who appeared on them. When my eyes came across one picture, I told the officer that was the man I saw. He asked me if I knew him and I said, No." He said "that's Oscar, Samir's cousin." "Then he asked me to testify before the court so that justice would run its course."

"Your testimony before me says that you saw the defendant handing money to Samir in a café. Will you elaborate?"

"I was sitting in the Café Naufara in Liberty Street downtown one day when Samir walked in and sat at the table opposite mine. I didn't know him then. He looked confused, glancing often at his watch and his nervous movements drew my attention. Only minutes later, Oscar came in and joined Samir in a short conversation looking around to see if anybody was watching. After a short while Oscar took out an envelope from his pocket and gave it to Samir who opened it and quickly put the banknotes which were in the envelope into his briefcase, took a file from it and handed it to Oscar, who left the café in a hurry, immediately followed by Samir."

The Judge asked Oscar to comment.

"Your Honor, I'm a peasant and never ever sat in a café and have not been downtown in years. I have never met this man in my life and don't understand what he is saying."

The Judge ordered the second witness to be called in. After the usual formalities, he asked the witness,

"What do you know about the defendant?"

"I know Oscar very well, Your Honor. He's been my neighbor for over ten years. He is in fact a good man but his behavior has changed recently, especially in the past year. He began to go out more often at night and bring back things hidden under his clothes. The improvement in his circumstances and lifestyle has been noticed by all his neighbors. He started paying much more attention to his looks than before."

"Did you see anybody visit him frequently?"

"Yes, Your Honor. There were two persons. One was Samir Plumber and the other is unknown to me. They both visited him constantly. I saw them leave his house late at night many times."

"How did you know one of them was Samir Plumber?"

"I know Samir quite well. We were classmates at the same elementary school. We used to meet quite often in Oscar's house before he deviated from his normal conduct."

"How do you comment?", the Judge asked Oscar.

"Your Honor, this witness is the officer who led the raid on my house the night I was arrested. He has never been my neighbor. I do not know him. I had never seen him in my life until the night he seized me and took me to the security department."

The presiding Judge conversed with his two aides in a low voice for a short while and announced the adjournment of the trial for deliberations. The three men discussed the case together at length. The presiding Judge started,

"Now that you have heard everything, what do you say?"

"The accused seems a simple and naïve person. I don't think he is related to that rogue organization. I also have some reservations about the two witnesses", said an advisor.

"But he admitted the charges against him, with his own signature on his confession.And confession, as we all know, is the best evidence," replied the other.

"Yet he said that confession had been forcibly taken from him under torture. The law cannot accept such confessions under coercion."

"Well, you know we have instructions to indict him. We do have secret evidence to be able to do so in addition to his own confessions."

"It is really ridiculous evidence! It is hardly even evidence".

"It is, after all, considered legal evidence. But let's leave the last word to the Judge."

As soon as the court was re-adjourned, the military usher's strong voice reverberated around the court room,

"All Rise." The Judge asked the audience to sit down. A few moments of nervous silence were broken as the Judge began to read aloud,

"Having listened to the Prosecution, the Defense and the witnesses; having read the secret evidence provided by the Prosecution and security apparatuses; having looked into the details of this case and after deliberation and in the presence of litigant parties, the Court has decided to sentence the Accused Mr. Oscar Plumber to life imprisonment with hard labor and to deprive him of all his civil rights, on the grounds that he was found belonging to a rogue organization plotting against the government. This verdict is deemed to be final and not objectionable by means of appeal or cessation. It is to be executed with immediate effect on the day of issue."

The shock was too heavy for Oscar to bear. He did not expect such a harsh, unjust punishment for something he did not do, something he didn't even know anything about. His only 'crime' was that he was a relative of a fugitive, Samir Plumber, who was wanted by the authorities and accused of agitating civil disobedience by urging people to claim their rights and freedoms.

* * * * *

Chapter Eight

President Markabandi, Head of the State of Obediestan arrived in the Republic of Illusion on a state visit. He was received at the airport by 'Chairman' George, his wife Marilyn, in her capacity as Prime Minister and all ministers and dignitaries. The reception reflected the noteworthy importance of the visit.

In the Hall of Honor, the Leader welcomed his guest with a typically ostentatious greeting:

"We warmly welcome you, Mr. President, in our Republic of Illusion, your second home country."

"I thank you very much, Your Excellency, for your highly appreciated welcome and hospitality."

The presidential motorcade moved straight to the Guest Palace, the official residence during visits by distinguished guests.

During the official dinner held in honor of the visiting Head of State, a number of agreements between the two governments and deals between CEO's from public and private corporations in the two countries were signed. An agreement to receive students from Obediestan to study in universities and colleges in the Republic of Illusion had been reached; sons and daughters of the rich in Obediestan preferred to study abroad, living in 'developed' countries and speaking their tongue to free themselves from the ethical constraints of traditions back home, as well as to be able to spend fortunes on sensual pleasures, such as parties and gambling.

The President Markabandi, together with his entourage, arrived at the Guest Palace:

"Your suite is ready if you'd like to have some rest, Mr. President. It's been an eventful day with very much accomplished," said the Presidential Chief of Staff.

"They say there are marvelous places here for amusement and entertainment. I feel like going out to see them," replied the President, pouring himself some wine.

"Yes, Sir. But we should seek advice on that from our ambassador here. He knows this country well."

"Good. Bring him to me now."

When called, ambassador asked bewildered:

"Mr. … I mean… the President wants to see me right now? Is there anything wrong?"

"Don't worry, Your Excellency. He only wants to acquaint himself with some places of interest and entertainment in this country and he trusts only you."

"His Excellency's trust is a great honor for me. But it is nearly past one o'clock in the morning. Most such places are now closed. Only casinos are still open."

"Then let me first ask him."

The Chief of Staff asked the now tipsy President:

"Sir, our ambassador says only gambling casinos are open at this hour. What shall I tell him?"

"Good, great. Let's go… and don't forget the bag! We'll need money!" the President cried cheerfully.

In the monitoring and eavesdropping room, one intelligence spy turned to his colleague:

"Check out what this moron is set on!"

"What do you expect of such people. You seem unfamiliar with their narrow minds," came the reply with laughter.

"He's for sure unaware that we're spying on him."

"Oh, sure. Perhaps he was told to feel free to do whatever he and his delegation wanted and no surveillance would be in place. But even our Foreign Affairs' officials know we cannot compromise our national security."

President Markabandi awoke the next day at noon, and after his breakfast asked his Chief of Staff:

"Did my son, Clever, call?"

"No, Sir, not yet."

"Call him then and find out why. He knows I am here."

Clever's mobile rang once, twice, three times... and no answer. The inebriated playboy was deep asleep in the middle of the day after having spent the whole crazy night with his mates screaming their heads off at a rock concert given by a local rock star.

Half an hour later, the aide called again. Clever's sleepy voice came through his heavy tongue:

"Wh... Who... is it?"

"Sorry, Sir, if I disturbed you. I'm your father's Chief of Staff."

"What do you want?"

"Sir, your father would like to see you before leaving the country tomorrow."

"Yeah, OK. Thank you for telling me."

Clever hung up without a clear answer. He got up, annoyed; dressed quickly and rushed to the Guest Palace.

On arriving, he hugged his father warmly:

"Welcome, dear father."

"Why didn't you call or show up? You know I am here only on a short working visit!"

"I'm extremely sorry for the delay, dad. I'm up to my ears in preparing for my final exams… look at me, I didn't have a moment's sleep last night studying till dawn."

"And where's your sister? We tried to call her many times in vain. I'm worried."

"Don't you worry, father. She's fine. But she can't return calls because she's in hospital…"

"What? What did you say? In hospital? Is she ill and I don't know?"

"Don't get upset, dad. She's just a little unwell but she'll be better soon."

"Alright then. Do you need anything?"

"Just wish me luck, dad."

"Tell your sister I miss her but I won't have time now to see her. Tell her to call me when she leaves hospital, hopefully soon."

Venus had been admitted to hospital three days before her father's official visit, after a sudden and serious loss of weight… she turned sickly pale and began to suffer from a complete loss of appetite and concentration, checking in as she didn't know the reason.

Clever visited his sister at hospital next day and was shocked when he saw a ghostly figure:

"What's this, Venus? What's happened to you?"

With tears on her cheeks and with a faint voice, she murmured:

"I don't know, Clever. I just don't know!"

He dashed off to the doctor's room:

"Please, doctor, tell me straight, what's wrong with my sister?"

"I'm sorry to tell you the initial lab tests showed that Venus is HIV positive."

"Are you saying she has AIDS?" Clever shouted in fright.

"I'm awfully sorry, sir, but it's true. Nevertheless, I promise I'll do my hardest to cure her."

Clever collapsed on a chair, his head in his hands.

* * * * *

On the third and final day of the official visit by the President Markabandi, a farewell party was held at the Fantasy Palace during which the two heads of state exchanged presents. President Markabandi presented the Leader with a sword of pure gold; the Leader presented his guest with a flag of the Republic of Illusion made of simple cloth:

"We thank you Mr. President for your visit and valuable present, and kindly ask you to accept our humble present in return."

"Thank you so much for your hospitality and valuable present. It is truly and deeply appreciated," replied President Markabandi humbly.

"We will be awaiting the day when you start to carry out all the agreements we have reached during your visit."

"Rest assured, Great Leader, we will soon. We are fully aware of our obligations."

President Markabandi was seen off at the airport by the Minister of Foreign Affairs: the Leader was too busy preparing for the upcoming presidential election within three months. Extensive high-profile meetings with influential politicians, financial and media tycoons from both local as well as international markets were part of his aggressive campaign, all at a time when a recent crucial opinion poll had shown his Socialist opponent was clearly ahead of him.

His popularity had receded lately because he failed to fulfill his promises before the previous elections. Instead, he had dedicated all his time ever since becoming

President to serving the interests of big corporations, making commoners into servants and even slaves to those organizations. Poverty, injustice and resentment rose rapidly to alarming levels; all areas of public life witnessed dangerous deterioration; the general situation in the country began to show menacing signs of imminent civil disobedience and, possibly, revolution led by the poor and the starving.

The Leader met with the giant multinational corporations' executives and top financiers, the wealth of each far exceeding the whole national budget of a developing country, in desperate attempts to muster their blessing and support in the elections. Exalting his wife Marilyn to the post of Prime Minister had had a great positive effect on her widely influential family.

At such a meeting, he began with phrases designed to remind:

"Gentlemen. You know I have kept all my promises to you all throughout my presidency. I don't think you'll find a better person to serve your interests. As you are aware, I'm sure, I am now urgently in need of your support for another term."

"Be sure of our absolute loyalty, our Great Leader. During your present term in office, markets have flourished and we've all benefited from lucrative business and made great profits," replied the Finance Minster, himself the owner of several major oil companies. David reiterated the Minister's words and promised immediate efforts to secure the Leader's re-election. Satisfied and flattered, the Leader replied, smiling:

"Thank you, David. The challenge lies in the diminishing public support due to general feelings that I have always sided with big businesses at the expense of the so-called 'masses'. My Socialist opponent has persistently focused on this point in his writings and speeches, accusing me of allowing capitalists to monopolize control over the wealthy resources of the country, of disseminating ruthless market values, and that our government's policy cannot achieve social justice or equity in the distribution of wealth."

He paused a little and went on:

"Public discontent was raised to crisis point by the death of some people who took medicines that were out of date and which had already gone bad. Our opponents also accuse us of siding with tobacco companies helping them kill more people due to throat and lung cancer and passive smoking despite our efforts to ban smoking in public places and transport."

"Let them accuse whoever they want and say whatever they like. At the end of the day, the decision is ours," said the owner of the giant Tobacco & Cigarette Co.

David, with his typical air of self-confidence delivered a short speech:

"We haven't moved to take action yet, Mr. President. We will soon set up committees with the task of polishing up your image, and others will have the task of smearing the Opposition. We'll probe deep into your opponent's past and expose his secrets and any irregularities, financial or otherwise... everything related to his family, wife, children, friends and supporter. We already possess a complete file on him."

With a sigh of relief, the Leader added:

"Thank you, thank you all for your sincere support. Now I can set my mind at rest. I'll be grateful to you for the rest of my life."

* * * * *

Days, weeks and months passed slowly for Maurice as he struggled hard to achieve the primary goal of his immigration to the Republic of Illusion – to be able send adequate sums of money to his mother to pay for the release of his father from prison. He worked as a cleaner in a restaurant fifteen hours a day, sweeping and cleaning the floor, clearing tables and washing dishes.

Despite the high cost of living, he managed, with his common-sense understanding of the simple principles of economy, to save a reasonable amount every month. When he finally thought the accumulated money was good enough, he sent the remittance to his mother back home. He felt he was the happiest man on earth when he heard his father was released from jail.

Things, however, did not run the same course for long. Suddenly, there was no news from him. He no longer contacted his mother – he used to call her twice a month to learn about how she, his sister and his father were doing. No calls came or news of him whatsoever for over a long month. His family grew extremely worried, particularly his mother who was prone to anxiety and delusions as she became obsessed by doubts and upsetting thoughts. Her heart was beating his name and his face was always on her mind as she prayed continuously for his safe return, soon. She began to confuse day with night and when she could not stand the painful burden any longer, she found a comforting outlet in listening to her sympathetic neighbours' who advised her to seek out a "good" clairvoyant in a farm nearby.

Women, they told her, go to the "wise" old lady for all purposes, from reading their future, to cast spells to bring their womanizing husbands back home or banish evil from their souls or their homes.

When Maurice's mother entered the waiting room in an old house in that remote farm, she found a group of women sitting silently stealing curious looks at each other. An old neighbour recognized her:

"Hello, Rhoda. I haven't seen you in ages. How are you? What's brought you here?"

"I'm here to ask the clairvoyant to tell me what has become of my son Maurice. I've had no news of him for a long time—over a month now!"

"Don't you worry, Rhoda. This woman knows everything. She'll tell you whatever you want to know about your son."

The short conversation had broken the awkward silence. Each woman suddenly became a talking soul; they began to tell their stories to each other, unaware of the presence of a secret undercover aide to the clairvoyant whose job was to entice clients to talk freely about their secrets and the reasons that brought them to the farm to consult her master. She normally pretended that she wanted to go out to spend a penny or to stretch her legs until her turn was up. She would then go to a back door and tell her master everything she had heard from the client who was next in line. The clairvoyant, in turn, pretended to gaze with great curiosity into her crystal ball, repeatedly encircling it with her hands murmuring magic words that gradually turn into intimate personal information, leaving her gullible client stunned and awestruck.

Soon it was Rhoda's turn. She was taken aback at the fearful atmosphere inside: a gray-haired, wrinkled-faced woman sat on a thick, woolen rug in the middle of a smelly, murky room lit by only one flickering candle, beside her a small brazier filling the place with thick fumes of incense.

The clairvoyant saw her approaching slowly and carefully. She asked her, sweeping the air around her ball with her heavily tattooed arms:

"Enter with your left... raise the curtain with a lift... Brrrrr... Sit in front of me... and listen to me."

The clairvoyant's ghostly voice made Rhoda feel more and more frightened and bewildered. She sat down in front of her and did not utter a word. The clairvoyant threw another pinch of incense into the brazier, and from behind a fresh wave of smoke and fumes, her sepulchral voice came out with a deep thunder:

"Brrrrr... Poor soul: worried mind... wrecked heart... all for your son Maurice. Don't worry... he will return wreathed in victory."

Maurice's mother couldn't believe her ears! How did the old woman know all this about her son—even his name?! She had not even mentioned him! Yet she was delighted to hear such comforting words about her son, and her sudden change of mood, from fear to delight, encouraged her to ask the old clairvoyant:

"Please tell me where is he now? Why didn't he call all that time?"

"He's been given a free hand... in a new land... He'll come back... with a gold pack... He'll bring you the best... and set your mind at rest."

Rhoda flew sky-high with joy. After paying the clairvoyant a generous sum, she hurried back home. When she arrived — exhausted— her husband was waiting anxiously. She had left without his knowledge and it was already very late. His eyes burnt with fire when she told him she had gone to consult the clairvoyant about their son:

"I can't believe your worry about Maurice would drive you to act in such a silly and naïve way. Why didn't you tell me before you decided to go there? If you had done so, I would have spared you all that unnecessary and unjustifiable effort. You know I don't believe those humbug tricksters. All clairvoyants are no more than a bunch of quacks and impostors... they know about our son nothing more than we do. You should've gone to Benedict's mother and asked her to call her son and ask him to bring us news from Maurice."

Benedict told his mother that he hadn't seen Maurice for over a month. That was normal in those countries as people worked from early morning and sometimes till late evening, so by the time they got back home they were normally utterly worn out. No sooner had they prepared dinner, they ate quickly and were ready to drop. He explained that normally he didn't have the time or oomph to pick up the receiver and call this or that friend. Maurice had already started a new job and had to take up residence far away from Benedict, and it was quite natural, therefore, not to have seen or heard from each other for over a month. Benedict, however, promised his mother to try to find Maurice's address and to discover why he had failed to contact his family.

"Hope what you've just heard will give you some relief," said Benedict's mother to Rhoda.

"I can't rest easy till I hear his voice with my own ears." replied Maurice's mother.

Benedict left no stone unturned trying to get news about Maurice, but all his attempts were without success. Yet he did manage to get a clue when a friend told him he had seen Maurice working in a restaurant in the outskirts of the city. The proprietor told Benedict he hadn't seen Maurice for over a month and that he didn't know the reason for his unusual absence. He advised Benedict to ask the police about his friend as he was residing in the country illegitimately:

"He was an illegal worker in my restaurant, that's why I couldn't tell the police when he no longer came to work or I'd be in big trouble."

"I only wanted to be sure first."

* * * * *

"Yes, what can I do for you?", the police officer asked Benedict.

"I'm looking for a friend. His name is Maurice Tailor. His family lost touch with him a while back and they asked me to find out if there's any news of him."

"Can you describe him?"

"He's brown, tall, black-haired in his early twenties."

"Do you know when he disappeared?"

"Not exactly, no. But he stopped contacting his family over a month ago."

It didn't take long when the officer came back with a file from which he took out a photo and showed it to Benedict. It was a photo of a young man lying on a blurred background with closed eyes. He looked almost like Maurice:

"Is this the person you're looking for?", asked the police officer.

"He looks very much like him… But I can't tell for sure!"

The officer held a small plastic bag and picked up a silver ring from it. He gave it to Benedict and asked:

"Have you seen this ring before?"

"Oh, My God! It is his ring. I saw it on his finger"

"I'm very sorry, sir. The man was found killed at a train station. His body is still in the morgue at the Town Hospital. Early in the morning of Friday, 15th of March, a taxi driver called the police and told them he'd found a body lying in a pool of blood. Police and the ambulance rushed to the scene and the body was immediately taken to the nearest hospital, but the man en route had died. The forensic report stated he had been stabbed six times. The police found nothing on him except a piece of paper on his chest with these words handwritten: "Filthy foreigners Go Back Home!" We couldn't establish his identity because he carried no ID or anything telling us who he was. Nobody came forward to ask for information about him, so we kept his case in our records under Case 456: Murder of unknown male with racial motives."

With a heart mangled with grief, Benedict called Maurice's mother to tell her of the tragic news.

The news came as a such a blow that, upon hearing it, she fainted.

Benedict made all the necessary arrangements to get Maurice's body transported back home and paid all costs in appreciation of their age-old friendship. When, eventually, the coffin arrived in the village, Rhoda threw herself over her son's body wailing in intense grief. Suddenly she remembered the clairvoyant's words and, through her sobs, cried out:

"She told me he will return safe, wreathed in victory … She lied to me… she … lied … to … me," repeated Rhoda deliriously, her voice fading.

* * * * *

Just as the shock of the events at the hands of the Judge had begun to wear off for Oscar, he found himself facing the nightmare of reality. He was jolted awake by the nerve-racking groan of his cell door opening. With a voice full of contempt and spite, the officer at the door ordered:

"Get up you filthy traitor… How can you sleep with your guilty conscience!" Then to the two guards behind him: "Take him to ward 17!" the notorious ward for inmates convicted of treason. he was dragged to the steel doors which the two guards promptly opened. Through a cloud of vile smoke which greeted him, one guard kicked him violently into the crowded ward:

"There! Meet your end with your fellow traitors, all beasts like you."

Oscar stood with his back to the door, and scanning the miserable wretches and wrecked souls, he began to feel suffocated by the morose smell. The ceiling turned dark gray and he noticed dirt strewn everywhere. In one corner of the immense ward lay some shabby, colourless rugs, seemingly used by fortunate inmates.

In no time, he found himself surrounded by a crowd of anxious and curious prisoners, bombarding him with questions:

"What's the situation outside?"

"How are people living? Are they satisfied or complaining?"

"Why are you here?"

"Have you been tried? What for?"

"How long is your sentence?"

He didn't answer any of the questions and didn't say a word. He felt his knees began to fail him so he sat down and wondered: "Will I have to serve my sentence with these men? Will they take me to another ward? Another cell?" Throughout this, images of his wife and children never left his mind: "How are they doing now?", he wondered with a sorrowed heart.

Frank, the eldest inmate, he seemed to be in his late sixties, "Uncle Franky", walked toward Oscar and patted his shoulder sympathetically:

"Don't be sad, friend, don't despair. We're all passing through the same ordeal, but we still have hope. Be optimistic. Don't let despair kill you!"

"What's your crime?", one inmate asked eagerly.

"Believe me I have no idea why I am here… I've done nothing wrong. A cousin of mine is a journalist and he might have written something against the government. They chased him everywhere and raided my house to force me to tell them where he was hiding. I honestly don't know where he is, and I kept on telling them that all the time but they arrested me, tortured me and finally sentenced me to life imprisonment."

'Uncle Franky' shook his head:

"We all live on hope here. Do you have children?"

"Three sons".

"You're not the only one. We don't know how our families and children are doing or what has become of them."

"What an outrage! What am I doing here? What are these innocent people, these prisoners of conscience doing here? What is the guilt of their families and children? When will this injustice end?," Oscar wondered to himself silently, his inner monologue interrupted by Frank's voice:

"Come on, you must have some sleep. They'll wake us at dawn and take us to work all day in a coal mine nearby."

"Do prisoners work in jail?", Oscar asked naively.

"Yeah. We're all sentenced to hard labour in this ward. That's why it is called 'HLW'; Hard Labour Ward?", answered Uncle Franky.

The inmates soon dozed off, exhausted after a long day of hard labour in the mine. Only Oscar's eyelids refused to close, his eyes remained open, his thoughts focusing on his wife and children... thinking of their ordeal after his arrest... and what the next day would bring for him.

* * * * *

Chapter Nine

In the remote mountains under heavy military protection lay the country's most crucial nuclear reactor and the adjoining storage plants. A specialized team of engineers were assigned there to work under exceptional security measures on a very sensitive project - the production of a new nuclear weapon with a highly destructive capacity.

"Come on chaps! Step up your oomph! We're in the final stages; soon we will announce this great scientific triumph. We're awaiting the Leader's visit to honor your hard work and reward you accordingly," the Chief Engineer told workers and experts in the plant.

He approached a busy engineer at his work station.

"How are things going?"

"Very well," replied the engineer, too engrossed in his work to make eye contact.

The Chief Engineer caught a glimpse of the screen the engineer was looking at and pointed alarmingly to one of the indicators.

"What happening there?"

"It's only a slight rise in the reactor's temperature… but there's no need to worry," replied the engineer coolly.

"Yes, it is only a slight rise, but it reveals a fault in the apparatus."

"Don't worry, sir. Everything's under control."

"Maybe, but if that worsens, we'll all be great danger."

"I'll try to discover the cause, sir, and put it right."

"Okay. Carry on. I'll be back soon to follow up."

The Chief Engineer completed his tour around the plant keeping abreast of the latest developments and giving instructions. No sooner was he back at his desk in his office than his secretary rushed in asking him to call the Minister of Defense without delay.

"What," he exclaimed, "the Minister of Defense? At once! Why didn't you call me on my mobile?"

"I did try, sir. But I couldn't get through."

He checked his mobile and found six unanswered calls from his secretary.

"Did he ask you to tell me anything else?"

"No, sir. I told him you were taking a tour around the reactor."

He promptly called the Minister.

"Sir, my secretary has just informed me that you wanted me to call you."

"It's not urgent. I only wanted to know about any progress you have made in the project."

"We're in the final stages, sir. The project is almost complete."

"Good. I also want to tell you the Leader has decided to pay you a visit at the laboratory before the end of the month. The visit is expected any day of the last week of this month."

"We'd be honored by his visit any time."

Before hanging up, the Minister gave his latest instructions. The Chief Engineer, in turn, called the plant's General Manager to put him in the picture.

Three weeks later, the Leader's awaited visit was announced. All hands were busy cleaning and decorating the plant with bright colored banners and the national flag. They raised slogans hailing the "Great Leader" and welcoming him on his visit. His picture was on display throughout the plant. The G.M. supervised all preparations himself and was under direct control of the "Chief" of Intelligence.

On May 28th, the special Protection Squad, led by the "Chief," arrived at the plant at dawn to make sure the place was safe and secure before the official motorcade approached carrying the Minister of Defence, Chief of Staff, Army, Navy and Air Force Commanders and other top brass who had to be there before the Leader to order to receive him.

All workers were outside, forming two opposite lines on either side of the entrance with the G.M. and the Chief Engineer at the head. Cheers and shouts of "Long Live the Leader" reverberated around the place the moment the Leader's helicopter landed. He waved back to the managers and workers who held up banners and placards carrying welcoming slogans and the Leader's famous proclamations.

The Leader, once having finished inspecting most of the huge plant with his entourage, headed alone with the Minister of Defense to the reactor where he was received by the Chief Engineer.

"You are most welcome, our Great Leader. It is a great honor to visit us on the site..."

"May I, Mr. President, introduce the Chief Engineer Koyoto," motioned the minister.

"Show me where you have got to in the project!"

"We are in the final stages, Sir. We will have completed the whole project within a month from now at the latest."

"Great. Carry on the good work."

"Thank you, our Great Leader for your generous visit."

* * * * *

One dark night, Samir and his group met again at that remote, shabby house to discuss the latest developments in the country. Only John didn't turn up.

"Where's John? Why didn't he come?" Samir asked.

"It's very strange," replied Julian, "He's never late. Something must've happened, I'm afraid."

"Let's wait a bit before we start the meeting. Perhaps he'll show up," suggested Samir.

"I say we cancel the meeting right now. If John is caught, we are all in real danger. He won't hold out long under torture and will reveal our names and our rendezvous," Neville warned.

Samir rose to look out through the window as he saw someone approaching, hoping it was John. Suddenly, he asked his colleagues to turn off the lights and keep dead silent until he was able to recognize the approaching figure. Everyone held their breath as Samir, through the dusty window and the darkness outside, observed the man pause a little, glance around and continue towards the door. Samir, recognizing the figure, breathed a loud sigh of relief.

"It's John. He's here."

"I'm sorry folks. There was a traffic jam because of an accident. All roads were closed and I had to walk the remaining distance to get here. I didn't take the normal route but thought it would be better to take a short cut across the fields, in case I was being followed."

"Thank Heaven you're here at last – safe and sound."

"I was so frightened when I saw the house completely dark. It looked so empty, with nothing to show that anyone may be inside. I was about to turn back."

"When you didn't show up we thought something bad might have happened. We took precautions and decided to cancel the meeting. We turned off the lights when I saw a figure approaching the front door, not knowing it was you. Anyway, let's start. We haven't got much time. Let's listen to what everyone has to say. Neville, you go first."

"They tested the spacecraft recently. The test seemed a success, to everyone's surprise."

"It's the biggest craft of its kind in human history. It's really quite astounding what it is capable of," Julian added.

"It's really an achievement, but in fact it is no more than a scientific luxury and a huge, deplorable waste of public money. Billions have been squandered on it whilst thousands die of starvation, disease and polluted drinking water," Samir commented.

"I believe they are preparing it for a specific and very important mission," said John.

"It's obvious and clear, comrades. They are preparing it to flee the country in case the situation runs out of control. What I can't understand is, why the gigantic size? They could've managed with a much smaller craft for that purpose," Samir thought.

"Firstly, I think it's megalomania...second, they can't survive on their own; they have to take their soldiers, servants, aides and even their property of theirs that is mobile with them," was John's comment.

"But where are they going to flee to?" Neville wondered out loud.

Samir replied, "Heaven only knows! What about the current tests on the new nuclear weapon they're working to introduce? According to the latest information I've got, it'll be the most destructive weapon ever produced…"

"You're right. If this weapon is ever used, it could wipe out the entire earth," Julian agreed.

"I think they're now in the final stages of the project. They may well have actually produced the weapon. Now, let's move to the next subject: what are people saying?" asked Samir.

"They are complaining bitterly…they're toiling day and night to pay back their overdue debts…some are tied up by banks and loan and mortgage lending institutions under severe terms and have found themselves working as slaves for these institutions until their debts are fully paid back, causing a significant rise in hardship as well as psychological problems and nervous breakdowns, including a jump in divorces and suicides. On the other hand, only a handful of people control these institutions and, through them, they ruthlessly control all the country's wealth. Many people are now on the verge of bankruptcy and collapse. They're being driven to desperation," explained Neville.

"Despair doesn't solve the problem, rather, it complicates it. We have to create hope and optimism for desperate people. Yet, more importantly, we have to create a sense of awareness in their minds," replied Samir.

"People are now beginning to see the merits of the Socialist system which they decided long ago to rid themselves of in favor of Capitalism. They were not aware that Capitalism and the Leader's regime are only two faces of the same coin. They only differ in their method of domesticating the masses in order to steal their wealth. The latest poll results reflect people's discontent very clearly – Bergisky, Leader of the Socialist Party, beat the "Leader" George by a very wide margin," was Julian's analysis.

Samir took over. "Our duty is to explain to the masses the true policy of this man who publicly advocates Socialism and declares his determination to stand firmly on the side of the poor in their struggle to get justice and fairness in the distribution of national wealth. But actually, as we all know, Bergisky himself is a leading feudalist— he owns a huge farm where a cousin of a friend of mine works and tells tales about Bergisky's capitalist mentality, his ruthless exploitation of the peasant farmers and his indescribable greed."

"Socialism and Capitalism, in my opinion, are again only two sides of the same coin – they are mere slogans created by politicians and business tycoons to serve their own interests," John added.

"I'd like to ask Neville if he learnt any news of my cousin Oscar."

"His trial was a blatant farce. He was sentenced to life imprisonment with hard labour. He was charged with conspiracy against the regime and membership in an outlawed organization."

"It's both a ridiculous and tragic irony that Oscar is a simple and humble peasant who never got involved in any political activity in his life, yet they brought those very charges against him."

"They have destroyed his life, and with such total indifference," Julian said deplorably.

"And they have the blatant shamelessness to proclaim empty slogans that they themselves don't even take seriously: Liberty, Justice, Equality. Neville, please add Oscar's family to the list of families entitled to our financial support, and together with John carry out the task of delivering the money to them without arousing any suspicion and without letting the family know the origin of the support. The meeting is now adjourned. Our next meeting is on the first of next month," Samir concluded.

* * * * *

Chapter Ten

The Chief Engineer was troubled on the journey back to his office. His thoughts searching for a possible solution to the unanticipated technical problem. His wife interrupted his train of thought, calling to remind him of the dinner party her brother had invited them to.

"Are you still at the office, Koyoto? Have you forgotten about the dinner party?"

"No, dear, I haven't. But an emergency is forcing me to stay here. I'm so sorry that I won't be able to make it to the party."

"What? What do you mean you're not going? What am I going to tell my brother and his wife?"

"You can go on your own, dear. Please ask them to kindly accept my apology and explain the situation to them."

"Is this to say you can't join us even later?"

"I've already explained. It's an urgent and dangerous situation. I'll tell you everything in detail when I get back home."

"That's enough. I don't want to hear anymore. Your work always comes first."

She hung up abruptly, not even giving him a chance to say good-bye. He slowly placed the receiver back into the phone and, putting his head in his hands, with deep sorrow, said to himself, "We stand worlds apart."

The telephone rang again, repeatedly, but he didn't go to answer. After a minute, his secretary rushed in:

"Sir, Sir. The G.M. is on the phone. It's urgent."

He quickly picked up the receiver:

"Hello… Yes, Sir!"

"I've heard alarming news. Is it true there is a fault in the pressure gauge of the reactor?"

"Yes, Sir. That's correct. We're trying our hardest to contain the problem. There's no need to worry."

"What if it can't be fixed?!"

"It must. I've asked all engineers not to leave. I will stay with them to supervise the repair operation and follow up developments personally… we will not leave until we make absolutely sure everything is alright."

"OK. Keep me informed at all times. I'll call you from home. And if necessary, I'll call the Minister of Defense."

"Thank you, Sir."

Koyoto swiftly put on his overalls and rushed to the reactor's control room. He asked the monitoring engineer to step aside and, taking his place, scanned the control meters and screens testing various buttons and keys. After over an hour, he turned his chair round and asked the engineer nervously:

"I think we've got a serious fault. Any suggestions?"

"I'd say we should stop the reactor and try to replace the pressure gauge with a new one."

"How long would that take?"

"A couple of weeks... we would have to ask the factory to manufacture it specially, as we have no spare devices or parts in the warehouse."

"But that would be too long."

"Even if engineers worked continuously day and night, I don't think they would finish the job in less than two weeks."

The Chief Engineer was furious. Slamming the control desk hard with both hands, he shouted:

"That's impossible! What will we say to the Minister of Defense? What shall we tell the Leader?!"

After five long hours of fruitless efforts to repair the serious fault, Koyoto returned to his office and asked his secretary to call all engineers and workers for an emergency meeting, then he called the G.M.:

"Hello… I'm so sorry, sir, to call at this late hour."

"It's alright. Have you fixed the problem?"

"I'm afraid we have to stop the reactor completely, sir. The problem is beginning to get out of control. We have to stop the reactor, otherwise…"

"Otherwise what?!", asked the G.M. furiously.

Koyoto paused searching for the right words to explain as tactfully as possible, though the G.M. didn't give him a chance and roared impatiently:

"I don't want explanation… I need solutions. This fault must be fixed using any means necessary… otherwise it'll be disastrous for all of us… understand?"

"Sir, the reactor must be stopped for several weeks to be able to replace the pressure control device… the situation is extremely dangerous."

Still unconvinced, though now calmer, the G.M. spoke:

"Let me think it over… keep trying… I'll call the Minister."

Koyoto had hardly put down the receiver when the phone rang again–it was the Minister of Defense this time:

"Tell me Koyoto, what's going on at the reactor?"

"Yes, Sir. There is a serious defect and it is now getting out of control."

"This sounds critical. Why wasn't I informed earlier?"

"I've informed the G.M., sir, maybe he's trying to get in touch with you."

"You tell me what happened."

"One of the engineering teams told me they were not able to contain a problem with the reactor's temperature and asked me to have the G.M.'s permission to stop the reactor for a couple of weeks till the problem is solved."

"Don't stop the reactor until you receive further orders from me. That is an order."

The Minister then called the Presidential Palace to talk to the Prime Minister, having realized the seriousness of the situation. He had informed Chief of Protocol that the Prime Minister had just arrived and had said he was not be disturbed under any circumstances. At the Minister's insistence that the matter can not be postponed, the Chief of Protocol called Marilyn:

"What's the matter, Danny? Do you know what time it is now?"

"I am extremely sorry. But it is so urgent; it can't be put off."

"What is it so urgent that can't wait till morning?"

With an embarrassed tone in his voice, Danny replied:

"The nuclear plant's G.M. told me, Madam, there's a fault in the reactor that has gotten out of control. The Chief Engineer asked my permission to stop the reactor for a couple of weeks. I thought I should consult you first."

"Don't listen to that little coward any more. He's of the type who's afraid of his own shadow. Give him orders to carry on as normal."

The Leader overheard the conversation:

"If it involves any risk, it'll be better to stop the reactor. We're not in a hurry. Patience is wisdom in this case."

She put her hand on the receiver and said:

"I'm not a child, George. Please let me bear responsibility for my decisions. You just relax, it's a trivial matter."

Then to Danny at the other end of the line:

"Listen. Do not stop the reactor. Follow up this personally yourself if you have to."

Danny immediately called the plant's G.M. and spoke to him sternly:

"Intensify your efforts and don't allow anybody out 'til the problem is completely solved. But do not stop the reactor. Do you get me?"

"Yes, sir. Understood."

Within a few hours, The Chief Engineer was filled to the brim with a mixture of fury and exhaustion when the telephone rang again. It was 3:30 a.m. The G.M. was on the line:

"Listen carefully to what I'm going to say. I've just received strict orders from the Minister insisting that we should not stop the reactor. You simply have to carry on. No one is allowed out. Expect a visit by the Minister any minute to oversee the problem first hand."

"But is he aware of the gravity of the situation, sir? Do people at the top know how catastrophic the consequences could be for the whole country if things got further out of control?"

"I've told them everything. Your only duty is to carry out orders."

Koyoto turned to the assembled engineers and spoke clearly, hiding his outrage and bewilderment at the orders he had received:

"I'm going to be frank with you—we are passing through a very serious crisis. Pressure at the reactor is too high and a catastrophic explosion may occur any minute. You all know the consequences. I want you to do your best to contain the problem. I have strict orders not to let anybody leave before the defect is fixed. The Minister of Defense may turn up any time to inspect the situation himself."

He then left to get back to his office, sadness mixing itself in with his other emotions.

* * * * *

In a family dinner held in celebration of her new appointment, Marilyn's parents sat with some relatives at the oval dining table engaged in cheerful conversation.

"I'd like to propose a toast to Marilyn who has her mother's beauty and her father's ambition. We congratulate her on her appointment to the top post of Prime Minister." her father addressed the family gathering. He looked to his daughter and said jokingly:

"From now on you are 'My little Dame'. I'll be proud of you as long as I live"

"My dream I have held so dear for so long has finally come true. Marilyn's always been a shrewd and sharp-minded girl—besides being so beautiful, of course! I, too, am so proud of you and will be forever, Marilyn," her mother said in turn.

"I am your child and you are the best of parents, and I will be grateful to you forever." Marilyn praised back.

* * * * *

Having toured the reactor site accompanied by the Army's Chief of Staff and formed a first-hand opinion on the extent of danger, Danny wrote a detailed report to the Leader on the latest developments at the nuclear plant focusing on the severity of the crisis and emphasizing the Chief Engineer's request to immediately stop the reactor until the problem was contained and the fault fixed.

The Leader read the report and, after moments of hesitation, added a note: "Referred to the Prime Minister for a decision and consultation. A copy of her comment should be sent to the Minister of Defense."

When Danny read the Leader's comment, he was amazed: "Has the Leader been deprived of any role or even opinion?! Is this all he can do even, though I warned him against the danger of not taking the magnitude of the problem into account? Was he even in command of his senses when he wrote this? How can he let her compromise the country's security when he knows damn well she lacks any experience in dealing with such matters?!" Nervous and raged, he called the Leader in a desperate last attempt to persuade him to intervene, hoping to settle the matter once and for all.

"Sir, I'd like to discuss the situation at the reactor personally".

"Carry out the instructions you were given, Danny. I don't want to hear anything more about the damn reactor. If you have anything to ask or request about this, then consult Marilyn."

"Sir, please give me a chance to explain the extent of the danger. I have seen the seriousness of the problem myself. It has far-reaching repercussions. If anything goes wrong, the whole country will be impacted."

"And why don't you tell Marilyn that? Stop overstepping her or her authority when it comes to the day-to-day running of the country." The Leader hung up abruptly leaving Danny no chance to utter another word.

* * * * *

An engineer, monitoring the screen before him turned and shouted out:

"This is dire. Sir!"

"What's the matter. What's happened?", asked Koyoto.

"Look, sir. The inner pressure has risen almost to the red. The reactor could explode at any minute. It is now completely out of control."

Koyoto rushed to the nearest microphone:

"Attention. Attention. All workers get ready at once for total evacuation."

Then he promptly called the G.M. and said in a frightened tone:

"The plant must be evacuated immediately, sir. The reactor will explode any minute now. The temperature is too high and the pressure in the nucleus is distressingly high."

"Stop the reactor at once. I'll take full responsibility before the Minister."

"It's too late, sir. Please give orders right now to evacuate the plant immediately. We are rapidly running out of time."

The G.M. had no choice. He gave the order and called the Minister:

"Sir, we can no longer do anything. The plant has been evacuated as matters have taken a turn for the worse. Only engineers were asked to stay and they're trying their hardest to control the situation by remote control from outside the reactor site."

He was shocked and couldn't take the news. He cut off the line and rang the President straight away:

"Mr... Mr. President, I'm sorry to tell you that I have bad news regarding the reactor," said Danny with sad voice.

"What's that?"

"The engineers lost control of it, therefore it might explode any time."

"What are you saying?! It's a real disaster? If the reactor exploded, it would be devastating! We would all die!"

"The only way out is to get the spacecraft ready. I can't see any other solution."

"Has it really got that bad?"

"Yes, sir. We must prepare the craft right away!"

"Alright, I'll give the order to get it ready as soon as possible. You, too, get ready and don't tell anybody about the reactor. Chaos is the last thing we need now."

At once, the Leader called Marilyn, who was still celebrating with her family, and commanded her in the strongest terms to join him in his office at once–the situation was extremely critical.

Leaving her parents' house in a rage, she rushed to the office where the Leader was waiting for her impatiently. On entering, she was shocked to see him pacing up and down the spacious office like a raging bull, looking disoriented and frightened. Still, she didn't try to calm herself down:

"What is that urgent and critical situation to disturb me for at my family's dinner?"

"Listen to me very carefully. The situation is terribly serious. There's no time for discussions or arguments… the nuclear plant is in real danger. The reactor may well explode any minute and if it does, it would destroy everything. If it happens, it would be fatal for the longest time, the uranium nuclear radiation and toxic gases would spread over the entire country."

It was all too much for Marilyn and she fell onto the sofa, totally stunned.

"What did you say?" she asked crying.

"We must act now! Crying doesn't help."

"What shall we do? Where shall we go?"

"I've already given instructions to have the spacecraft prepared. This is the right time to use it."

"I don't believe it... is it that bad? Who's responsible?"

"You are the only responsible person for the whole crisis. In spite of all sincere and genuine warnings, you tried to convince me it was only an exaggeration fabricated by my brothers to muddle up your recommendations and responsibilities. Anyway, this is no time to blame or criticize. We have to rush to the craft. Tell your parents and I'll tell those who should be with us on board."

"Do people know anything about this?"

"No. I've asked Danny to be discreet about the whole story."

Walking in quickly, Danny briefed the Leader:

"All set—the craft has been supplied with enough nuclear fuel to operate it for many months. The crew has already started the engines. I've just left the soldiers filling it with food, drink, as well as all other necessary supplies for the journey. I told them some top officials and ministers will be taking the craft for a test journey and will be in transit for some time."

During this time helicopters dropped water on the reactor to cool it down as they attempted to prevent it exploding.

* * * * *

Chapter Eleven

Angela sent a lunch invitation to Brian, which gave her brother a sense of pleasure and happiness that he had not felt for a long time. He realized that it was the first time he had ever received such an invitation from his sister.

Brian rang the doorbell with his elbow because both hands were full of presents for Angela and her husband. Brian's sister received him with warm, open arms.

"Believe me Brian, your visit is a precious gift for us," Angela said, receiving the expensive presents and leading her brother inside.

Brian was particularly pleased with the sight that awaited him; three courses of his favorite dishes were set out on the table.

"It wasn't really hard to work out, Brian," Angela said. "I often heard mother warning me not to touch any of these meals. 'They are Brian's favorites,' she used to say. Her words stayed with me, and now, finally, I have the chance to prepare them for you myself. It's been a dream of mine ever since you left, and you can't imagine how happy it makes me to see my dream come true. Come now. Bon Appetit!"

Brian felt a strong, strange desire to ease himself of the heavy burden of remorse. He knew he had a hand in his father's passing and wanted to get closer to his sister, and maybe in this way he could also help alleviate some of her deep sadness. He began to talk about their childhood and seemed eager to learn about what had happened since he had left to start anew, particularly about his parents.

"You know, Brian," Angela said. "Your name was on father's lips when he was dying. He wanted you by his side before his last breath."

"I wish I could turn back the clock, so that we could stick together as a family and I could ask him to forgive me," Brian said.

"He did forgive you," Angela replied. "It's true, I heard him with my own ears. Mum reminded him of you, and she cried on my shoulder when she, too, heard him speak your name, praying for your safe return."

"Thank you, Angela," Brian told her. "Thank you so much. Now I can set my mind and soul at rest. What about mother? How did she manage after our father passed away?"

"It was hard for her," Angela said. "You know how close they were. But she didn't forget you a moment. She also wished to see you before she departed this life."

His only response to hearing this was the flow of burning tears streaming down his face.

* * * * *

Koyoto's voice rang through the PA system.

"Attention! All staff, evacuate the site at once. Repeat: Evacuate the site at once."

The G.M. was monitoring the situation through the CCTV screens, and as soon as he heard Koyoto's warning, he immediately called the Minister of Defense at the Leader's office.

"It's over, Sir. It's the end… the disaster. We have no choice but to evacuate the reactor's site. All attempts at repairing the faulty operating and control systems have failed. We are in a race against time, and, frankly, we're losing. The explosion is now inevitable—it's only a matter of when. We have no more than a few hours at most."

The Minister looked to the Leader, and both turned to Marilyn.

"It was the plant's G.M. The explosion, he says, is imminent. The reactor won't hold long."

"Ask the Cabinet to convene for an emergency meeting," George commanded.

"I can't even stand," Marilyn replied.

George was relieved to find Danny close at hand. He asked him to call for an urgent meeting and to include army and police commanders.

The officials showed up with grim, bewildered faces. The manner in which the meeting was called was highly unusual, even for an emergency, and they immediately suspected something dire was afoot. Not a single one of them had dared to imagine they would have to leave their palaces, farms, all their belongings, their positions of authority and set off, sooner than they thought, on a journey that would leave everything behind them.

The Leader came in feeling no less wretched, and looked around the room feeling depressed and disappointed. Feigning composure, he began:

"Listen to me carefully! We are facing an extremely serious situation. I want every one of you to have the courage and confidence to find a solution, our country needs this. You all know about our endeavor to produce a nuclear weapon more powerful than ever. Well…"

The Leader paused to wipe the sweat off his forehead and swallowed hard.

"Well… regrettably, things have gotten out of control at the reactor site and it will most probably explode at any time now with devastating consequences: widespread destruction, fatal radiation and serious threat to all life in this entire country and beyond. Yet, we've taken some precautions and had the spacecraft prepared for a special and historical mission. We have decided to mount a getaway mission, and all gathered here will travel on the ship, away from earth and into space, where we will remain until the danger has subsided and it is safe to return. Now, we must all prepare immediately for any eventuality and for our escape."

The group looked at each other with pale, shocked faces. The rumblings of chaos had begun to appear when the Leader motioned Danny, signaling him to begin his brief on the craft.

"This spacecraft is fully equipped and furnished to the brim to cater for your utmost comfort and luxury during your stay. It's an airborne city and at every street corner you will find an info center with an explanatory map of the inner sections of the craft. In short, all your needs will be catered to. Our journey, I can assure you, will be as comfortable as possible."

The Leader noticed no visible reaction from Danny.

"The craft is also equipped with a full Defense and Assault system," the Leader added. "Powerful missiles are ready to automatically deal with any attack we may encounter, designed to hit enemy targets with unprecedented precision. Our genius engineers have invented a luxurious world inside the craft, and on the outside, an invincible flying fortress."

"You will now go to get your families ready for the journey. I ask you to take special note of a very important order I must give. Do not, under any circumstances, communicate to anyone outside of this room the reason for our urgent preparations and journeying. With the confused situation we are already facing, anarchy is the last thing we want or need."

* * * * *

Within an hour, the Republic of Illusion turned into a bustling hive— multitudes of cars and other vehicles raced against time at to get ministers, top officials and officers, business tycoons and their collective families to that metal haven in time for departure. A special highly trained squadron directed the traffic, arranging for entry and guiding the families to their allocated places.

The giant engines started roaring within minutes of Danny giving his instructions to get the craft ready for takeoff. After the Leader, Marilyn and her parents had boarded through their special entrance, the crew began the countdown.

Those left behind included members of the Presidential Guard who were ever ready to sacrifice their lives defending and protecting their Leader. Unaware of what was actually going on, they remained dutifully in their positions. They were lead to believe that the Leader and his entourage were making a leisurely tour of the spacecraft.

* * * * *

All indications inside the reactor showed without a doubt that the explosion was getting dangerously closer second by second. The alarm amongst the team monitoring their screens closely swelled toward breaking point. Although the reactor was being monitored remotely from an underground centre, one engineer couldn't help shouting.

"Look," he yelled. "The temperature and pressure gauges are jumping wildly into red levels. There is nothing we can do now. We shouldn't even be here."

"You're right, but I have yet to receive instructions to evacuate," replied Koyoto, feeling increasingly disorientated.

"Instructions?! This is suicide. We have no time. We'll not sacrifice our lives waiting for instructions!" cried out one engineer defiantly. Koyoto realized he had no choice.

"OK. Get ready to leave. I'll tell the G.M."

There was no answer from the G.M.'s office. Koyoto then tried to call the Minister.

"I'm sorry to tell you, Sir, we now have no choice but to evacuate the reactor's site. Things are completely out of control. We desperately need your permission."

"What?", Danny screamed, "Aren't you on board the spacecraft yet?!"

"No, sir. We've been busy doing our job, but we've failed, I'm afraid. And I've been waiting for your instructions or permits......"

Before he could finish, the Minister at the other end heard a deafening explosion and the line immediately went dead.

An ear-splitting explosion jolted the whole area, shaking the streets and squares of the Capital as a dense, foreboding black cloud of smoke began to cover the skies. Red-black fireballs soon shot high into the grim sky before raining down, spreading lethal radiation and deadly gases.

Danny watched as he sat in the cockpit, his co-pilot at his side. Any second now he would receive the Leader's takeoff order. The gigantic metal beast started roaring with an indescribable pressure, leaving all nearby buildings trembling and smashing windows as far as miles away. The slow uplift stirred storms of white smoke and clouds of dust as the craft's rockets ignited with tremendous power. In what seemed an instant, the craft soared away into the open sky with a deafening, menacing boom.

People in the earthly Capital were terrified by the combined horrifying explosions of both the reactor and the takeoff; too frightened to even begin figuring out the source of the disturbances as the skies darkened. Soon, however, word got out and they ironically came out, filling the streets chanting, clapping and cheering.

Chapter Twelve

Having broken clear of the atmosphere into the endless expanse of space, the craft began its flight at its peak speed. Passengers were frightened at first, but very soon their nervousness lessened and they began to relax and enjoy the steady, smooth cruise through the empty stretches of space. The state-of-the-art equipment on board gave them a sense of reassurance and faith in their vessel. They even began to delight in their environment, walking freely around the "flying city."

As scheduled, the Leader's voice was heard by his guests through the tannoy.

"It is my pleasure to congratulate you for your safe escape from an imminent disaster that would have killed us all, had we not had the foresight to prepare for the worst. Now, I'd like you to enjoy this privilege of traveling into outer space, available only for those like yourselves, who are extremely affluent and fortunate enough to have this experience in their lifetimes. Our journey may last several months. We will eventually return to Mother

Earth, once any danger from the radioactivity has been absolutely and completely eradicated. Bon voyage, and God bless you all."

* * * * *

Those remaining in the capital of the Republic of Illusion began taking desperate, last-minute precautions to head off the imminent and inevitable nuclear danger. When the inhabitants realised the terrible explosion they heard was not only the roaring sound of the spacecraft's engines, but also the sound of the nuclear reactor blowing up, the radioactive fragments were already forming a thick, dark, and deadly cloud, covering the skies above their city.

Adam rushed out to try and discover what was happening. He turned quickly back to his wife, Angela and her brother, Brian:

"The nuclear reactor has exploded!"

"What? Adam! An explosion at the nuclear power station?! How do you know? It would be an absolute catastrophe" shouted Brian.

"Yes, it is a catastrophe."

Brian tried to contact some of his high ranking friends through his mobile to get some more information, but discovered all lines were dead.

"Don't bother, Brian. I heard people say all top officials are already on board the craft with the Leader and his junta. They've fled and left us here on Earth to face our macabre fate."

"The villains! Murderous crooks! They've robbed the country of its wealth, and now they flee!" Brian was fuming over the perilous predicament.

Merciful Heaven, though, suddenly intervened. The initial raindrops were to be the first in a downpour that lasted for days. Within hours, the fires at the nuclear plant and nearby woods were extinguished by the rainstorm, as gale-force winds began to drive away the deadly mushroom cloud, propelling it away from the city and scattering with it the nuclear dust and radiation. Two days later, the rainstorm came to an end as suddenly as it had begun, and people were able to get out of their homes, unable to believe that they were still alive and no longer in mortal danger.

* * * * *

A determined crowd, cheering as they were led by Samir, marched to the central prison and persuaded the guards to free the inmates, since the ruling junta had fled on a journey of no return.

Relatives and friends hugged and kissed each other warmly, joyful that their ordeal was finally over. Those who were told their loved ones had either died and been buried in the cemetery nearby or just disappeared stood aside broken hearted and upset by their helplessness, unable to do anything but cry silently.

Oscar elbowed his way through the crowd to see if his wife and children were amongst those gathered. Suddenly, he heard a familiar voice calling him:

"Oscar! Oscar, we're over here!"

There they were; all of them. He held them tight, all at once between his arms kissing each again and again – having been so afraid that this wish could never come true.

They were leaving the homewards when they heard a feeble voice calling:

"Oscar… Oscar..."

Oscar didn't recognize the old disabled man in the wheelchair.

"I want you to forgive me, son!"

"Pardon me ! Do I know you? Have we met before?"

"You know me very well, Oscar. Look at me well and you'll remember..

Oscar stared at the wretched man, still unable to recognize him.

"If you have forgotten me? I haven't forgotten you. I am the reason why you went to jail! I am the Judge who sentenced you to life imprisonment. I am the reason that you were separated from your wife and children. Do you remember me now?"

Oscar was totally shocked: He remembered the strong, tall, conspicuously respectful gentleman with a very loud and confident voice. Yet, before him was a sickly, disabled and paralysed man—a thin, pale-faced ghostly figure with unkempt hair and beard.

"If you are that judge, what happened to you to become so miserable?"

"It's God's punishment, my son. If one deserves it, He may postpone it, but He will never forget. Unlike human punishment, Heaven's is always in kind."

Then he started telling his story.

"The same day I gave you that sentence, a truck driver lost control of his lorry and hit my car. He and my chauffeur died instantly. I woke up in the Central Hospital to find my legs had been cut off and one eye lost, as you can see. I wished I had died that day – I didn't only lose my legs and an eye in the accident, but my job, too. After I left hospital I thought long and hard about my conduct and actions, and about the verdict and sentencing that day. I felt you were innocent—in fact, I was sure! But, I was carrying out orders from higher authorities. Again, I felt that was no justification. I was living in a state of delusion—I couldn't comprehend the sense of injustice. Now, I have realized my guilt, and I am here upon advice from a good friend of mine to see you and ask you to forgive me, so that I can set my conscience at rest."

With an affectionate hand-shake, Oscar told the old judge:

"Ask your conscience to forgive you. For my part, I bear you no grudge… I have already forgiven you."

* * * * *

Chapter Thirteen

People on board the spacecraft quickly got down to their normal every day routines; meeting each other, exchanging views as they dined together, discussing projects, having fun, and treating the journey like an extended cruise. Before too long, however, boredom set in as the journey itself became more and more monotonous. And soon it was no longer exciting or even amusing. Those on board suddenly felt a yearning to walk on 'Mother Earth,' To experience the seasons again, whether it be   the hot sun of summer or the cold rain and snow of winter. They began to miss strolling in the parks and commons, stretching out on the green grass, breathing the fresh natural air, and listening to bird song.

Three months after leaving Earth, the Leader suffered a severe heart attack and rushed to the on-board state of the art hospital. He was under close observation in the intensive care unit, and grew weaker day by day. His health showed obvious signs of serious deterioration.

While traveling through space lying in his hospital bed in a weakened condition, the Leader began receiving fewer and fewer visitors. Once it became certain he would not survive another crisis; he finally found time to face himself, open his life's book, and look back at its eventful pages. For the first time in his busy life, he realized the extent of injustices he had carelessly committed against so many people while seeking to serve his own selfish interests. The extent of corruption he had spread in all government departments through his decrees had served only the interests of greedy business tycoons and corporations. He looked around, feeling the pain of plastic tubes inserted in his nose, mouth and veins. Being kept alive in the I.C.U. only by life support machines; friendless and powerless. He felt alone and lonely.

"How trivial and silly our life is. Its little pleasures are sheer illusions. Its sweet joys like dreams. One day I possessed power, authority and fame. People rallied around my name loud and strong. Where are these people now? Here I am dying alone, not even my wife in attendance. I spent all my life doing everything, literally everything, for that women to satisfy her every selfish and reckless whim. Where is she now? Having fun, as usual, with relatives and friends away from my deathbed! How could she be so cold and ungrateful?" he lamented.

He was incensed at the thought of Marilyn and her perfunctory visits which became less frequent as the weeks went on. Each time she acted as if she was reluctantly performing an imposed duty. He could clearly feel her nervousness at his bedside; always impatient to leave and get back to her crazy lifestyle. He remembered his brother Michael's advice and regretted not taking heed at the time. He was now at the stage where if the illness allowed and he lived long enough; he was intent to dismiss her from her post and replace her with his brother Lewis. The worst fear, however, was that she would replace him as president and Leader if his life was cut short by this sickness.

His mixed feelings of regret, remorse and self-criticism were stopped short when Marilyn's strong fragrance revealed her presence. Recently she had bizarrely begun to pay much more attention to her looks; making extra efforts to wear the best perfume and the chicest clothes and jewelry. Remembering how she had never appreciated his qualities in his heyday as a man, a husband, or a President; he wondered why she was showing such weird behavior now that he was a sick powerless man on his deathbed.

He looked at her meaningfully, and she got the message. There was a sense of guilt in her manner, almost as if she had a conscience.

She asked him in her typically coquettish tone, "How are you today, dear?"

"As you can see... getting worse," was his abrupt answer.

She looked away, breaking eye contact, maybe to avoid his stinging look. At this, he couldn't help but break down and cry:

"It's been a week, a whole week since your last visit! I haven't seen your father for quite a while, either. Where is he?"

"Sorry, George, " she replied coolly, "we've been busy celebrating my mother's birthday last week. I was receiving guests and my father was preparing for the occasion."

"That's the reason, then?"

She already knew it was a lame excuse, so she attempted an apology.

"Believe me George, I always thought of you and talked about you with my parents."

She paused, draped one arm around his neck, and with the other she subtly managed to switch off the pacemaker's control.

"Soon you'll recover dear. We'll celebrate your next birthday with great joy…"

"Stop being too optimistic. I don't think I'll ever recover." With a deep sigh he went on, "I've wasted all my life dreaming. It's time to depart this life. I can feel it. The journey of illusion I have spent with you is over. I'm glad I was disillusioned. I can see clearly now."

She feigned a cry and said, "Come on, George. Be strong and firm as we know you. Don't give up. I love you. We all love you."

"Get off me, you cheap liar! I was never happy with you. Our entire pretentious life together was a farce. And here I am, dying somewhere in endless space because of your greed, ambition, selfishness, miscalculation, and misjudgment."

She was completely astonished. He was never so direct or blunt with her. Never had he dared to upset her in any way or manner until now. She managed somehow to swallow her anger, aided by seeing his face turn deathly pale. She knew his final breath was coming shortly. These were crucial decisive moments in her life, she told herself, so she must try to be patient and calm.

Keeping her true feelings in check, she said, "Let me call your doctor. Your illness is taking it's toll on you and you don't know what you are saying. You need to rest, right now. You shouldn't exhaust yourself by talking."

"I know exactly what I am saying. What I realized today I have never comprehended before. The magic has now lost its charm; you're no longer the woman of my dreams because you yourself have shattered them."

He had to stop there—he suddenly felt tiredness and weakness overcoming him.

With his tongue growing heavy he managed to stammer, "I… I'll… d-d-is-miss…"

He wasn't able to finish as Death took him and those were his last words. His eyes stayed opened, his gaze staring around the huge cabin and out into space. It seemed to follow the spirit of his soul, now free to roam the heavens. His journey of illusion had finally reached its end.

Marilyn gave a sigh of deep relief. She switched the pacemaker's control on again and called the doctor.

"I'm so sorry to inform you, ma'am. The Leader has sadly passed away."

"What?!" She screamed. "What did you say? Passed away? How could the Leader die?!"

With typically feigned sadness and grief, she began to wipe her face with her silk handkerchief. The doctor stood there trying to find some consolatory words.

* * * * *

The Leader's sudden demise was sure to aggravate the already problematic relationship between his brothers and his widow. They had not been at all happy with her conduct from the very beginning, and had opposed her appointment to the post of prime minister. Though being certain of her inability to lead them, they had been unable to voice their concern to their late brother They knew that he was complacent and blind where she was concerned. Instead, they had chosen to remain silent in order to avoid any conflict.

In a private room, the three brothers held an emergency meeting, as was the norm in such a situation, especially after the passing of the head of state.

Danny started angrily, "George made a terrible mistake when he appointed her as Prime Minister. Following our statutes and constitution, she has now become our President and leader. This is a very serious and grave crisis in which we find ourselves. She lacks even the basic qualities and political experience necessary for leadership as she has proven many times."

Lewis commented in a rather accusatory tone, "That was my opinion from the very beginning, remember? But you failed to stand by my side when I spoke out openly against her appointment, even asking me to refrain from speaking my mind publicly. You have to take some of the responsibility for the crisis we are now facing."

Danny warned, "We must do something to stop the ongoing disaster. Blaming each other for this or that won't help us now. We are no longer on our planet where we exercised considerable control. We are here, careening though the vast expanse of space on an aimless journey into the unknown, all because of her crazy ambitions and foolish stubbornness!"

He paused and shook his head in despair.

"I can't imagine how this stupid woman managed to convince George to yield to her whims and demands! She foolishly insisted on keeping the nuclear reactor going in spite of all the dire warnings of our expert engineers. Now our world faces catastrophic repercussions brought about by her actions. When I warned George about the consequences of her reckless decision; he shouted at me! It was the first time in his life he had ever spoken to me in such a tone. Both he and Marilyn didn't budge an inch. Even after I submitted a written report. We could have avoided this disaster. Now we don't know what has become of our city, or even the extent of destruction it has suffered."

"I think we better leave things as they are until our return to Earth. I feel it's not wise to start a row with her now while we currently find ourselves adrift in outer space," concluded Tony in a rather low voice.

Marilyn could clearly feel the change in the brothers' attitude towards her. She decided to dismiss all of them from their posts once they returned to Earth. She knew some top army brass who were eager for promotion. They simply loved to be decorated with medals and badges and serve their own interests and political ambitions. She was intent to fully exploit this; especially since some of them had approached her with explicit wishes to gain her favor, if and when, she became Leader. She knew they lacked all respect for her and appreciation of what she had done, but as many believe, the ends justifies the means.

Marilyn called The Pilot for a special meeting. "From now on you answer directly to me and no one else, and keep me briefed immediately on all new developments. By the way, how are things going in the cockpit?" she asked.

"Everything's fine. But you know, ma'am, we have been flying in space for almost four months now, and have consumed a lot of fuel. We must, therefore, soon begin our journey back to Earth or at least make a stopover on a nearby planet to save on fuel before setting off again for Earth."

"How long will the remaining fuel last?"

"At least three more months, ma'am. Then we'll have no choice but to use the reserves.

"And how long will the reserve fuel last?" she asked.

"Two months, more or less," he answered.

"Great, we still have enough time."

"Whatever you say, ma'am. But I suggest we start our journey back to Earth as soon as possible."

"But you've just said we can stop at a nearby planet, haven't you?"

"Yes, ma'am. All I'm saying is that we better be prepared for gradual descent towards Earth."

"Go back to work now. You'll receive my instructions in due course."

* * * * *

Marilyn ordered an urgent meeting to discuss the suggestion of returning to Earth as soon as possible. She favored the idea of direct gradual descent.

"I've called you to exchange views about going back to Earth. The pilot told me we still have fuel enough to fly the craft for about three more months in space before starting to use the reserves. As you know, we left Earth four months ago. Since we don't know what has become of our country. I'd like to consult with you about this," she explained.

"I think four months is long enough for fires to stop and for the radiation to die away. Therefore, I suggest that we start our return at the earliest opportunity," Lewis said.

They all nodded. This, however, surprised and upset her. She didn't like Lewis and it seemed his suggestion caused them all to agree, which by her perception diminished her authority and leadership.

With typical pretension she replied, "We still have enough time. Therefore, I suggest we land on a planet at our leisure, giving us more time. Once we need to, we can continue our journey back from there. There's no need to hurry."

To which the Finance Minister readily agreed, "That's the right and sound suggestion. The later we return the more certain we would be of avoiding the effects of the nuclear blast."

Danny, however, frankly warned, "The craft travels at an exceptional speed. We don't have estimates about the force of gravity of the planet on which we will land or its impact upon the craft. We may well collide with force against the surface if we depend upon the wrong calculations."

Her reply was quick and sharp, "Why are you so pessimistic? The craft is capable of landing on any planet, any surface; you personally said it is equipped to tackle every conceivable difficulty in any situation. Don't forget you were granted a medal for Best Inventor because of these assertions. Now you say it may well run into the planet because of gravity!"

"Yes. The craft is equipped to function under all circumstances, but why risk trying something with unpredictable consequences? Unless, of course, there is an emergency. Besides, the majority suggest we return directly back to Earth," Danny explained.

At that point, she ended the meeting with a stern conclusion, "Thank you all for coming. Currently, I feel it is better to reconsider returning directly back to Earth. I've decided to land on nearby Mars; and after staying there for the duration of one week, resume our journey back home."

She paused and looked around at their faces trying to gauge their reactions. By insisting on a decision, even though she knew it was wrong, she hoped to prove she was the Iron Woman, the undisputed Leader, the supreme decision-maker.

* * * * *

Having concluded the meeting with her decision, Marilyn retired to her bedroom feeling distressed. For no apparent reason she began thinking back on her life, trying to figure out the reason or reasons for her unhappiness. She grew up in a wealthy and influential family, the one and only spoiled child of caring and loving parents, the undisputed and unrivaled little princess. This life had made her selfish and narcissistic. She wanted to possess everything for herself and was simply incapable of sharing anything with anybody else. Her ambitions knew no limits, despite the fact that she was now the Leader.

She took tablets to lighten her mood and tried to rest but found herself lost in an inner dialogue trying to alleviate her misery.

"Why am I so unhappy and distressed?! I should be the happiest creature on earth... in the whole universe! I've got all I want. All my wild dreams have come true. I am envied by all women, literally all women. So why do I feel so miserable? Is it true that happiness is just an imaginary ghost? Is it, as they say, that happiness cannot be bought by money or luxury?" she wondered.

She tossed and turned in bed, unable to sleep. Suddenly, her thoughts found a new track. She remembered her decision to land on Mars.

She thought it over carefully and wondered, "Did I make the right decision? What if Danny was right? Will we all end up lost forever in the wild, endless space? Will I lose everything I have fought for my entire life just as I have become President?!"

She sat up in fear and confusion. "What will they say if I go back on my decision? Will they think I am a weak woman, incapable of making sound decisions?" she wondered. She set about trying to find a way to resolve the dilemma she had created for herself. She realized her decision had been arbitrary and thoughtless. She too, wanted to go back to Earth quickly and directly, but Lewis's suggestion had pushed her into making a rash decision that was quite contrary to her own desires. Yet, she thought, it was the first decision she made as President and Leader. Going back on it now would destroy her leadership and make everyone view any future decisions with total disrespect and disregard. In the end, she settled her mind and convinced herself that she would never go back on her decision, whatever the cost.

* * * * *

The next morning she called Danny and gave him the order to land on Mars. On his way to the cockpit, Danny stopped to have breakfast with his brother Lewis and tell him about Marilyn's orders. Lewis had expected as much, but was still taken aback.

"What a stubborn empty-headed woman! Let's do what she says for now. When we get back to Earth we'll have a bone to pick with her," Lewis stated.

"That's what I'll do. Her outlandish behavior is really driving me crazy. I feel I'll lose my temper pretty soon and end up giving her a piece of my mind in front of everyone before we even reach Earth. Anyway, I'll leave you now. I must supervise the landing myself. See you soon" Danny said.

He set about examining all meters, counters, and gauges on the control panel; fuel, speed, altitude, inner and outer pressure and temperature, etc. He scanned the data and pictures sent back from the probes they had scattered over the surface of Mars years before. All devices were functioning perfectly. He then proceeded to the flight deck and slipped into the cockpit to check in with his assistant. He also checked the space around the craft through the watch-windows and monitoring screens. He received, in turn, data and pictures through the cameras fixed on the craft to indicate direction, corridors, and traffic, etc.

"How is it going?" Danny asked the pilot.

"Everything's under control, Sir."

"Do you think it is wise to land on Mars?" asked Danny.

"You know better, Sir. Yes, we can, but it's still a little risky, I feel."

"Alright then. We'll start gradual descent shortly. I'll handle it."

Danny took his seat behind the control board and made this announcement, "Ladies and gentlemen, attention please, we'll soon begin our descent towards Mars for a short stopover before resuming our journey back to Earth. Please follow all security and safety instructions when you hear those relevant announcements shortly. Thank you."

He started giving directions to the crew, "We'll go round Mars first, before starting gradual descent for the planet."

Then he explained, "We've been watching and monitoring Mars through digital transmissions from probes on the planet's surface. The images are highly accurate. Together with the digital analyses of all necessary data, we have been able to ascertain every possible safe landing site in precise detail. We should be very careful and alert. We're traveling at great speed around Mars. We will only start descent procedures when we are absolutely sure we can land safely."

"Sir, look. There on that screen!" shouted a crewman pointing to a blurred spot on one monitor. "These objects should be some high masses like our hills and mountains on earth."

"I guess you're right. We know Mars is the closest planet to earth in terms of landscape, atmosphere, and life supporting conditions. Even volcanic mountains and polar ice." Danny went on, "You have to take into consideration the difficulties and challenges we're going to face just before landing. The hardest part will be the planet's gravity, which will affect our attempts to reduce velocity as we land, but hopefully that will not pose too much of a challenge."

With full alertness, he surveyed the monitors before he called the new Leader.

"Ma'am. I'd like to inform you we will land on Mars shortly. We're now circumnavigating the atmosphere preparing for touchdown when we will complete the maneuvering operation," Danny reported.

"Good to hear. I hope everything is going smoothly."

"Yes, ma'am."

"Great, great. Stay in touch and keep me in the loop constantly on any progress," Marilyn requested.

"Sure, ma'am."

The spacecraft had completed a full circle around Mars when Danny gave the order to start the step-by-step descent maneuver. Over the tannoy, he made a final announcement to passengers to get ready and follow the necessary instructions.

Suddenly, the pilot shouted in panic, "Sir, the speedometer appears stuck. We are maneuvering for the descent and should be moving steadily onto the landing site. I'll try the emergency lever."

Seconds later, he shouted again, "The emergency lever is not working. This could be extremely dangerous, Sir."

"Try it again! It's a matter of life and death."

The pilot tried nervously many times to use an additional emergency lever, but all his efforts were in vain. Then, with a cold sweat of panic on his face, he turned to Danny and asked permission to use emergency brakes.

"Come on, use the damn brakes. We have no time to waste," Danny replied. Unfortunately, the 'damn' brakes failed to function as well.

"Nothing seem to be working, Sir. There must be something wrong somewhere," the pilot said in a panic.

"God! What's this?! The steering lever is dead stuck. We have no choice now but to fire the deceleration balloons", shouted Danny in total confusion and dread.

The crewmen shouted and cheered as the central speedometer slowly lowered to indicate controlled velocity as soon as the giant balloons opened above the craft. But their cries of triumph didn't last long.

Danny's Assistant cried out, "Sir! Sir!" his eyes bulging from alarm, "the speedometer is rising again."

With no more last resorts, Danny called Marilyn, frightened and furious at the same time.

"We've completely lost control of the craft, It will soon crash into Mars. It's all over!"

The Leader's tone reflected her horror.

"Don't say that Danny. Do something. Do anything… I don't want to die on Mars. Change course toward earth. I don't want to…"

"This is the price of obeying your crazy orders!" Danny interrupted and hung up.

She called him back instantly, but he didn't answer. Danny's voice reached all passengers for the very last time.

"It's the end! The Journey of Illusion is ove…."

He didn't have the chance to finish his message. The Craft finally hit the planet with a tremendous impact. The collision turned it into a fireball. Hundreds of tiny fragments along with countless human limbs scattered wildly into the vast, wild space.

Samir woke up, shocked and trembling. A rooster crowed, heralding the dawn of another new day.

~~~